MANLIO ARGUETA

A Place Called Milagro de la Paz

Translated by Michael B. Miller

CURBSTONE PRESS

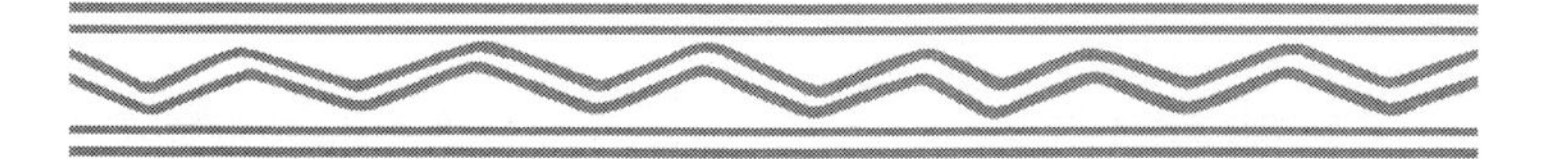

FIRST EDITION, 2000

This translation is based on the 3rd Edition of *Milagro de la Paz,* Adelina Editores, San Salvador, 1996.

Printed in Canada on acid-free paper by Transcon Printing / Best Book Manufacturing

Cover design: Les Kanturek

This book was published with the support of Worth Loomis, as well as the support of the Connecticut Commission on the Arts, the National Endowment for the Arts, and donations from many individuals. We are very grateful for this support.

Library of Congress Cataloging-in-Publication Data

Argueta, Manlio, 1935 -
[Milagro de la Paz. English]
A Place Called Milagro del la Paz / by Manlio Argueta; translated by Michael B. Miller.
p. cm.
ISBN 1-880684-68-3
I. Title.

PQ7539.2.A68 M5513 2000
863'.64—dc21 99-086170

published by
CURBSTONE PRESS 321 Jackson Street Willimantic, CT 06226
phone: (860) 423-5110 e-mail: books@curbstone.org
http://www.curbstone.org/

Translator's Acknowledgements

I wish to thank Dr. Edward Hood of the Department of Modern Languages at Northern Arizona University for his careful reading of the text and subsequent suggestions and Manlio Argueta for his helpful insights during the translation process. And, to my publishers, Alexander Taylor and Judith Doyle, for their encouragement and faith in the universality of literature, I express my deepest gratitude. I also wish to thank Gallaudet University for funding my travel in 1996 and 1997 to consult with the author and visit the barrio in the story where he grew up and stand at the foot of the Chaparrastique volcano, to see a fence of live pina, the stone fences built of volcanic rocks stacked one upon the other, the lavadero, the pozo, the fogón, the colorful tombillas, and the overall magnificence of the landscape of El Salvador. And to my wife, Margarita, for her encouragement and support, I owe so much. And to Leo Kanturek for his wonderful and imaginative cover design which so captures the spirit and the essence of the story, I am also deeply grateful.

To Adelina, my mother, who from the time I was a child cultivated in me great sensitivity, reciting to me out of her prodigious memory poems of love and of an exemplary life

A Place Called Milagro de la Paz

THE TWO WOMEN sleep together. It's their custom, before giving in to slumber, to talk about things that went unspoken during the day. In the darkness of the room, having their eyes open is no different from keeping them shut.

There's also a little girl in another bed.

They can't sleep. They've spent the hours before dawn listening to the dogs barking, a howling that's more like the sound of children wailing. They're barking at the men who patrol the streets to keep order in their barrio, but mostly it's the sound of their boots against the cobblestone pavement that sets the mongrels off, half-crazed.

That's how it is at night, the mother tells herself. *It's best if a person can just sleep.*

The daughter says nothing and turns over on her back. *She sees I'm really awake*, she tells herself.

The mother's *fustán* provides her the necessary warmth in the chilly morning hours.

"We're all alone here, but at least we're alive," the mother says. *I can hear a song going around in my head*, she tells herself. The words speak of yellow flowers that brighten the paths leading up to the volcano. Her thoughts about the dogs interrupt the melody. It is night and she wonders if they're howling out of fear, or at the soldiers who patrol the barrio, or at *los seres desconocidos* as they are called, faceless assassins who in recent days have been dumping dead bodies into Calle de las Angustias—the Street of Anguish.

Or maybe it's because the mongrels go to bed hungry. Magdalena: *I know when I go to bed hungry I'm more afraid.* It sounds as if their very howls are devouring the house.

Then my mother crosses herself and glances over to see if her mother is still awake. Magdalena bites down on her lip. It hurts. *In sleep there's no pain,* she tells herself. That's what her mother has told her. She stretches out her arms to feel about in the darkness. "Mama, mama, are you asleep?" Magdalena's imagination tells her the dogs have climbed over the stone fence and will soon be on the roof. "Nothing's going on. It's our imagination," Latina tells her. "Maybe it's death coming for us," the daughter replies. The mother: "Stop making such a fuss!"

It's all because of the soldiers. They never sleep. They go about at night—patrolling from midnight to dawn—keeping watch over the streets of Milagro. That's what makes the mongrels so frantic. The soldiers chant patriotic slogans and shout orders to boost their morale and make themselves feel more macho.

"And what if it isn't the dogs howling?" Magdalena asks. Because in recent months Milagro de la Paz has been invaded by packs of stray dogs. And with their long snouts they look like coyotes. Others say it's really some *unknowns, faceless assassins,* going around imitating their sounds. "I think we're safe here. We'll feel better if we can get some sleep," the mother says. Besides, the animals can't get inside the property because it's surrounded by barriers: barbed-wire in back, a high stone fence on each side, and in front, facing the street, a row of thick *piña* with thorns like needles.

"Do you mean to tell me those howls are all in my head?" Magdalena asks, her eyes half-closed, heavy with fatigue. Their fear is heightened by the fact that they feel trapped. The night—a shroud of frightening shadows—is a cloak that closes around them. Magdalena tries again to fall asleep.

Latina: *I think about my other daughter, Crista. She's little yet and lies there in the bed next to ours. I even think about Plutón, stretched out there at the foot of her bed.* Plutón is their dog. He doesn't howl or make a peep. As long as no one makes a sound, he just lies there like some dried up old stick. Magdalena has fallen silent. *What will become of them*? the mother asks herself, lying there, thinking about her two girls. For some mysterious reason she believes one of her daughters is going to die before she does. *At fifty-three I'm already an old woman and my time is past. I'd trade my life to save one of them.* She crosses herself to scare away the evil thoughts.

Magdalena turns over in bed to lie face down. Wrapped in her white sheet smelling of rattan, she fidgets impatiently. *I'm so tired. Oh, dear God, let me sleep.* They say if a person really wishes hard enough for something his prayer will be answered.

One last howl from the coyote-dogs is heard above the fence. *When I hear them, it seems like they're just outside the door, but they're really not. And when it sounds like they're far away that's when they're really close. That's how they fool a person,* the mother thinks.

And then, with some emotion: *Stinking* coyotes, *why don't they go to hell once and for all, and leave us in peace*? Suddenly the howling stops. *They can hear what a person's thinking, that's why they've finally shut up. For as long as we live in this barrio we'll never have a moment's peace.*

Magdalena detects her mother's thoughts and her breathing: "Go to sleep, mama. It's late." She moves over closer to her. The mongrels that roam the barrio at night had stopped their barking. But, the mother still won't get any sleep.

The only time a person doesn't feel any pain is when he's sleeping. I bite my lip and feel pain. Then that must mean I'm really awake. In spite of everything, within a few minutes she is snoring like a tired old god.

MAGDALENA, the older daughter, leaves the house every morning to peddle their merchandise to the rural folk who come into town. Clothes her mother sews at home, garments she herself has been gradually learning to make. While Latina sits at the sewing machine, Crista helps with chores around the house. All three share the work amidst the loneliness of Milagro de la Paz, where the only thing that breaks the silence of the days is the tower clock in the marketplace, striking the hour. *Lord, which of them am I going to lose?* Latina wonders. *If any of us has to die, let it be me.*

"Even if I pretend I'm brave, mama, I'm really not. I'm scared," says Magdalena. There are moments when she feels desperate. "Then sing," Latina advises her. "If I sing to myself in the dark, you'll think I'm crazy." *And my mother tells me:* "Just imagine how terrible it would be if you really were, and that's how it'll be if you don't give your head some rest." Magdalena: *And she taught me to sing quietly to myself, inside my head; that way, no one would make fun of me; I hum songs while I work; even when I go to bed and when I get up.* "That's life, mi hija."

"Singing won't help, mama. The truth is a person's life just slips away." Latina: "The one who sings scares off his troubles."

"Mama, what makes you say they're unknown beings and not *coyotes*?" Latina: "Because *coyotes* don't howl like that." She thought the animals had abandoned Milagro de la Paz. "The cotton pickers have been killing them off," she tells Magdalena. A sleepy silence. Then: *Should I wake Magdalena?* And I wake her. *She tells me to go to sleep, that there's nothing going on, that the soldiers who keep watch over Milagro de la Paz scare the mongrels.*

"WHY US? I don't know," Latina says.

"The night is like a mistake, an illusion."

Maybe it's because everything becomes a blur and the innocent get punished no matter what when the law is cruel. Latina: "Why are we always getting blamed for something?" The only ones who don't get blamed for something are infants at their mothers' breasts. Latina: "Sometimes I think something's going to happen to us." Magdalena pats her mother's hip to reassure her: "When a person's expecting the worst, nothing happens. Bad things only happen when we least expect them. It's called misfortune." Nothing was going to happen to them as long as they stayed together and "because God is great." *I can hear my daughter's heart beating even when I'm sound asleep. I hear Magdalena singing to herself.* Magdalena: *I tell my mother the night is more than a mistake. It's a nightmare.*"

Magdalena's ruminations are interrupted when daylight comes. Then she goes out to make her rounds. A farm couple approaches her and asks to see the clothes she is selling. "How much is it?" Either to haggle or to compare. When she grows tired after a whole day on her feet, she sits down with her basket on a street corner the campesinos pass by on their way to the market to sell their crops, or on their way to the town's main plaza or the church. "If you want, you can pull on it and you'll see how strong the seams are," she tells them. She is proud of the quality of her mother's work.

Except for Saturdays and Sundays, and popular festival days for the saints, the sales are meager and her hopes are bleak. She remembers what her mother has always told her: *You have to work if you want to eat.*

Magdalena: "Did you make sure the doors were locked tight?" *And I get up to see for myself. My mother says I don't trust her enough.* Latina: "Yes. Not even Saint Peter himself could pry open these doors." *Los seres desconocidos aren't going to attack us. Faceless murderers, they start their damn howling after midnight.* "No one can get in as long as we've got these doors locked." My mother sets out a *huacal* filled with salted water to keep out the evil spirits. It's a secret she learned from her great-grandmother. She was convinced that any evil spirit that might sneak in through the cracks would dissolve in the water, although we knew better. It would never keep a real person out.

Latina: *I've always believed in the mystery of things.* "The coyote-dogs went away," the mother says. Magdalena: "I'm not so sure because the howling I hear sounds far off, and that means they're really nearby." Both women are scared. *My mother says it's natural for people to be afraid. It's all because of "original sin".* "Let me get some sleep or else we'll be up all night," the mother says.

Ever since the soldiers who keep watch over the city had targeted the barrio of las Angustias for carrying out their military exercises, Magdalena's mood has changed. The mother tries to ease her mind and tells her to put her trust in the heavy wood beams that secure the doors. Besides, Latina has faith in her prayers and in the small bowl of salted water.

"Why do we need the soldiers here?" Magdalena wants to know. Outside a strong wind is gusting and it begins to rain. The unknown beings run for cover. "So we can feel safe," the mother explains. *I heard the mongrels jump over the stone fence and take refuge nearby in the town dump. The imagination plays tricks on us. I hear the coyotes howling all over the place, not just around our patio. They prowl about and can pounce on any of these houses. My daughter tells me again*: "Go to sleep, go to sleep." But even in sleep, the howling can be heard. "Maybe they're men disguised as animals," Magdalena says. *I begin to pray.* The daughter is sensitive to any sound: "I can even hear their voices in my sleep, even though you don't believe me," Magdalena adds. "Or animals disguised as men," the mother corrects her.

Their fears will vanish with the morning sunrise, but still over the course of the day they won't be able to stop them from resurfacing. *It's because our souls are so fragile,* Latina thinks. "Anyway," the mother says, "it's better for us not to remember the bad things that happened. Or else we'll end up making our lives a living hell."

The older daughter ponders the words her mother repeats everyday: "Hija, why were we born weak?" And I tell her: "We're strong. If it weren't so, we wouldn't still be here."

Magdalena: *Crista is the only one who's weak and that's because she's still just a child.*

SCATTERED WORDS, bits of laughter, sighs, laments.

"I like it when you're asleep next to me; it makes me feel better. I pray for you." The mother never grew weary of telling her older daughter why she was afraid: "It's because you don't pray at night before you go to bed. That's why." The day ends too quickly and the frightening dreams don't stop even with the arrival of a new day. *My mother decided that the best thing for us to do was to sleep together. My little sister sleeps in another bed, close to ours, with the dog next to her. That's how we're able to get some rest. We keep each other company.*

The mother feels better as a result of her prayers and *in having my two daughters close to me. The older we get, the more we're afraid of things.* The younger sister could sleep more peacefully because of that nearness.

Every once in a while Magdalena touches her mother's buttocks. It makes her feel safe. "I'm never going to leave," Magdalena says. She means taking up with a man one day and leaving her mother and younger sister alone. "Nothing can separate us."

The older daughter is thinking about that day when, on her way home, she found a bouquet of withered roses lying in the street. But their stems were still green. She marveled at the colors. Magdalena placed her basket on one arm and with both hands slowly brushed the dirt from the flowers. She is thirteen years old and believes it's time for her to begin thinking about the future, but that's something that still seems so abstract and remote to her, even though she is at the turning point in her life. Just waking up to a new day—that was the future. But, she didn't know that yet.

"Look what I found," Magdalena says, holding out the fresh stems for her mother to see. "There's enough here for us to start a garden." "That's the last thing we need around here. To bother ourselves with some flowers," her mother replies. "At night you give me strength, but during the day you're different," the daughter protests. Latina says life is more real in the light of day. The night doesn't exist; what exists are its horrors. "I'm going to plant a garden and you'll see. You'll help me and we'll grow roses." With some *caca de gallina* and water in the morning and afternoon, the rose bushes took root.

"THE TROUBLE with you is that you're always thinking the worst," the mother complains to Magdalena. *I can't help it if I'm scared at night, but she doesn't understand me.* Latina: "You need something to help you get rid of those bad thoughts." Magdalena tells her she doesn't need anything: "You're all I need." "You also have your little sister, and the dog. We're a small family, but strong; we'll survive." *I don't want to listen to her. There's always going to be something that scares me.* "Tell me, so I'm not left to wonder. What is it that has you so scared?" "It's just a feeling I get sometimes," she explains. *My mother tells me that premonitions don't exist, that they're just evil spirits that have to be rooted out of our minds.* Latina says it biting her lip because she, too, has a premonition about one of them dying, but she won't say it. "It always helps to pray," she says. *I tell her I'll probably never be a religious person and that's how I'll die.* "Don't say such a thing. It's a sin to talk about dying." An unforeseen death is the only thing the mother fears. "Or maybe it's just that I respect it. I can't explain it to you. All I know is that no one dies at vespers," my mother tells me. "The thing that scares me most about dying is that there's a great darkness," I say. *My mother says there's no darkness there, just a great light.* "Of course, it's a different kind of light," she says. "I don't know where you get that stuff from, those strange ideas," I tell her. "To overcome your fears you've got to talk about them," she says.

"Mama, why are men braver than us?" She answers me: "They've made all that up, but at the moment of truth, they're bigger cowards than we are!" I tell her: "Mama, sometimes you scare me more with the things you say. I know from what I've seen that our lives are in their hands." She answers me: "It only seems that way, hija. Illusions deceive. What's in their hands is death." *And I begin to tremble and I cry in silence so she won't hear me sobbing.*

MAGDALENA attends the school run by Doña Rafaelita, who also happens to be one of the town lesbians. At first, she rebelled, especially because of the distance. She had to walk almost a kilometer along the hot, steamy road. And then all the way back home, starting out at eleven in the morning, *the hour of the devil* when the inferno-like heat blankets the town of Milagro de la Paz and the asphalt highway melts and forms big reflecting pools.

By the time she completed her first three months of lessons, Magdalena already knew how to read and write, to do numbers and count. And later the mother tried very hard to convince her to quit when she was in the third grade. She was especially concerned about her daughter having to cross that street at the end of Calle de las Angustias where they dumped the dead bodies. She didn't like the idea of her daughter coming face to face with the reality of her nightmares. "If I didn't have two mouths to feed, I'd keep both of you locked away here, safe with me."

The mother accompanied her for the first week of school so she'd gradually become familiar with the streets and their dangers. She also put the teacher on notice: "And I won't have you punishing her, not with a stick across her bare bottom, none of that. When it comes to the children, the only ones to see them with their pants down is their family." She'd rather her daughter remain ignorant. The teacher stood her ground: "Without punishment, I can't be a teacher to them. You have to understand, I need to make the children learn and how can I do that if their parents don't let me punish them? There's nothing evil in punishment. Don't you see? Why, even God punishes." The mother reconsiders; maybe the teacher was right. "Well, if she needs to be punished for something, then go ahead." And the teacher knew that no child would dare consider a slap across the bare backside an unjust punishment; no one had ever complained to her. Because the little creatures would never tell their parents they had their pants lowered for a slap across their bare bottom. "Magdalena is smart. The best thing for her to do is to finish her primary schooling. Leave her with me for two more years," Doña Rafaelita told the mother. Latina unwillingly agreed to let her older daughter finish the sixth grade. "Well, I don't put much stock in all this learning or in people with a lot of schooling. I'd rather you tell me she knows how to look out for herself in this world." The teacher explains to her that's what school is for.

"AND WHAT'S this idea of the *infinite*, anyway?" Latina asks Magdalena. But she answers her own question: "I imagine it's just like the sea."

"No," Magdalena corrects her. "It's something much greater than the sea. It's as big as the distance from here to the stars."

And Latina can't believe the sea could be smaller than the distance from her home to where the stars are. The older daughter explains to her that the sea is only so big and that it can be crossed in a boat, while not even a four-engine airplane could reach the sun. She is astounded to see how much Magdalena knows about so many things; but, to her mind, none of it serves any useful purpose. She tells her mother that those are things she learns in school everyday. She even won first prize: the teacher rewarded her with a cutting of cotton fabric to make a dress. "Take it home to your mother to show her. Tell her you earned it with your brains and your sweat." It was her reward for having written all the numbers up to one hundred thousand. But once she finished primary school, she would have to let Crista, the younger daughter, have her turn. "Both of you have a right to some education, but I can only manage one at a time." That's when Magdalena began going out to work, making her rounds of the streets of Milagro to sell her roses and the clothes they made at home, while her mother stayed glued to the sewing machine and Crista attended class at Doña Rafaelita's school.

THE MOTHER and her two girls walk along the highway that takes them home. Latina, to protect herself from the hot sun, covers herself with a black shawl that falls over her shoulders and around her body.

"Why did you come looking for me?" the older daughter asks, addressing her mother and younger sister. "Because you were late coming home and I was afraid something happened to you." They continue making their way along the road, three figures slowly dissolving into the asphalt's shiny lake until, beneath the bright sun, they become completely invisible to the human eye.

THE OLDER daughter, on returning home from her day's work—selling roses and the clothes her mother makes—reprimands her younger sister because she has found the pots nearly empty; there wasn't enough water for the garden. "And all because you didn't haul up all the buckets of water we need. You spend most of your time in the house. There's no excuse." The younger sister explains why she didn't do what she was supposed to; it rained early in the day and so she saw no need to water the garden. And, anyway, there was already enough water in the pots. An unexpected midsummer rain. Magdalena answers her sharply, saying that it's just her excuse for not doing what she was told to do. "I might as well do it myself," she says even though she has come home worn out. Crista just ignores her. She has learned to use her eyes to communicate and express her moods. *She's got the eyes of a cat when it's stalking its prey*, Magdalena thinks. The younger sister meant to take care of it for her. *But I tell her not to bother. After seeing the way she glares at me, I'd rather do it myself.* "You've got to learn to pull your own weight here, because gazing at the stars isn't going to put food on the table," she says angrily. *I'd like to be as carefree as her*, Magdalena thinks, alluding to her younger sister.

The two sisters almost never share the work that needs

to be done. *But, when it comes to my roses, I'll go into a fit if I have to. I'm the one who did all that work in my spare time.* Crista goes on about her business. Even though they have different personalities, both sisters are strong, slim, and good-looking: the nose, slightly broad and flat; full lips, heavy eyebrows, dark complexion, sinuous body, agile movements. A penetrating gaze. They can be tenacious when it comes to their survival, but they're afraid, too. Ever since they were little, they've seen death on the prowl and they had to learn to be careful.

In the late afternoon, when the sun has gone down, the younger one goes to bed under the *nance* tree, on a bed of yellow leaves, and she begins to count the stars according to the order in which they appear, something she can do easily enough when there are only a few and she can keep track of them. She also knows how to count up to a hundred thousand like her sister Magdalena. But suddenly all of the stars come out at once and her mind isn't agile enough to keep up with them. Besides, it's time to go inside—to avoid the *suffering souls* that start coming out of their hiding places at night and also to escape the mosquitoes and the *jejenes,* the gnats that feast on a person's flesh. The only one the insects don't bother is the mother who some time ago took up smoking cigars, Honduran tobacco brought from Copán by Doña Matilde, the owner of the corner grocery store. At four in the afternoon she lights up and doesn't take it out of her mouth until late at night when she is ready to go to sleep, all the while puffing away like the chimney on a wood-stoked locomotive, like the one that brought the three of them from Usulután.

"While I'm out working, my sister is here daydreaming," Magdalena says. "Don't complain. She'll grow up soon enough and then she'll have to take your place," the mother retorts. Once the older daughter has taken the buckets to the well and finished fetching the water she needs to fill the pots, she turns sad. Magdalena feels guilty for having scolded her little sister like that. She has learned how to deal with Crista's personality, but there's always something that defies explanation. The mother tells her it's a family trait. That's how the grandparents were: fickle, strong-willed. "I don't think they sat around counting the stars," Magdalena protests sarcastically. "They couldn't even count the fingers on their hands, but they were hardheaded right up to the day they died." *Maybe that's why we're the only ones left. No one survives very long acting like that.* And the mother trembles when she wonders if maybe Crista will be the one who is going to die.

Magdalena: *It's that time of night when the bats come out and zoom around overhead. I stretch out my hand, wanting to catch them in flight. My grandparents died when my mother was still young.* It's also that time of night when the owls come out; during the day they perch themselves in the cemeteries; then, at night they come out and cast fire from their huge eyes. *I know, even though mama doesn't say it, that my grandparents died at the hands of the unknown beings.* Magdalena draws closer to her sister. *That's why we came here from Usulután.* Crista-child lies face up, stretched out on the ground, on a mattress of yellow *nance* leaves. "I'm sorry. I didn't mean anything by what I said," Magdalena says. "Let me be. I want to be by myself; I'm counting the stars and I've only reached five hundred, five hundred one, five hundred two..."

BY THE TIME she turned fifteen, Magdalena began changing and she started to overcome certain fears, too. She met Nicolás, a young neighbor who lived adjacent to them, on a plot larger than theirs, where his family grew *guineos* and pineapples. Their relationship turned intimate without their families' knowledge or permission. It was a love no one could know about, because at that age, confused feelings can breed sinful acts. And evil too. If two young people love each other, they have to keep it a secret. Their intimacy unfolded in stages, becoming a reality several months after they started seeing each other, a full two years after they first met.

My mother finally accepted it, unlike his family which wasn't about to stand for him becoming involved with a family of women. Women of no importance, women who had nothing except a small plot of land. What's more, they were different. Women who lived alone and stayed to themselves. "What would become of our son, a *varón* living there with three women?" his family asked.

And when I tell my mother about it, she says this is what happens when a boy and a girl make the mistake of falling in love at such a young age. Besides, his family was counting on him marrying into a family with a decent piece of property and all we had to offer was a little plot of land with some hens, a sewing machine, and this house we'll be paying for the rest of our lives.

Magdalena tells her mother that she loves Nicolás, and Latina asks her if she knows what that word means. The older daughter doesn't know exactly, but she tries to explain the best she can. "Love is when you feel little butterflies fluttering around in your stomach." The mother tells her that's true, but a girl has to know when it's time to tell those butterflies to go to hell.

Then one day Nicolás and Magdalena find themselves lying together in the hammock, under a faint half-moon, and her skirt slides up over her hips, revealing her youthful, mahogany-colored skin, as fresh as new wood. She draws her legs up to prevent Nicolás from getting on top of her. She feels confused. *Why does the woman have to be underneath*? she wonders. At a time like that, a girl needs someone who can properly advise her, but Magdalena has to be patient, not rush into anything, especially girls like her who have nothing to offer.

The mother had also been a woman alone. Widowed at a very young age and faced with the impossibility of staying on at Cerro el Tigre in Usulután, she had packed up and moved to Milagro. Magdalena was just a little girl and Crista an infant. "They murdered my parents. Who knows for what reason?" That was the only time they traveled by train. The tradition of women alone. "We're leaving. There's nothing for us to do here." They came by train from Usulután to Milagro. "What happened to our grandparents?" Magdalena asks. "Some men killed them. No one knows who they were," the mother replies. "In the *war*?" "No. In a struggle for a scrap of bread." Latina: *Death is such a familiar face to us, always on our heels until it overtakes us.*

MAGDALENA and Latina took turns selling their roses and clothes on the streets of Milagro, with the younger daughter always accompanying one of them along the way. "I'm going to teach you how to sew. That way you won't need to depend on some man just so you can eat. You'll never have to go hungry," Latina told her older daughter. For Magdalena it seemed strange that when it was her turn to stay home by herself she didn't feel afraid the way she did at night. Maybe it had nothing to do with anything inside the house, but rather the night shadows and *los seres desconocidos. I prefer being here by myself when my mother and sister are out selling our merchandise. I like to stay home and sit down to do my work at the sewing machine.* That way she could enjoy some solitude, something she found so pleasant because it afforded her the opportunity to fantasize about faraway places, other worlds, even if at times they seemed unfathomable mysteries to her, worlds she only knew *because of some books I keep underneath my bed.* Perhaps if she had had more time to read, she might have been able to decipher the perplexing geography of distant places. "The only time I read is when I'm by myself, out there in the privy," she tells her mother. "To know the world you've got to be out in it, there on the street, and you've got to learn how to use your hands for something," her mother repeats. "You won't learn any of that from books. A person has to know and understand people, how to talk to them." Magdalena would leave the house by herself to sell their wares, and when the little sister's time came, she would also have to do the same.

On weekdays, it's Crista who accompanies the mother on her rounds. On Saturdays and Sundays it's Magdalena's turn. "I like working at home better. That way I can sing whenever I want." The mother: "You won't learn anything about life if you spend all your time inside these four walls."

SHE HAD other reasons for wanting to stay home. She had met Nicolás. A chance encounter. The boy had come by to ask for some water. "Our well went dry," he said. By the time she was twelve, Magdalena began to have dealings with the campesinos but never with the people from the barrio, not even with Doña Matilde, the owner of the grocery store, because her mother took care of everything they needed. Nicolás represented her first warm relationship with a person other than her mother. After three weeks, they became friends, and after several months strong feelings developed between them. But she had been taught that love at her age was wrong, even sinful, and so she tried to avoid seeing him. "My mother won't accept you because your family has some property and you grow bananas and pineapples. As for us, all we've got is this sewing machine and some hens." The poor with the poor and the rich with the rich. An unwritten law, but it only seemed natural. "And we've got this house we'll be paying for until Judgment Day."

As the months passed, they became intimate with each other. It came after a number of chance encounters and some flirting. Whenever Nicolás walked past their patio, on his way to the well, Magdalena couldn't take her eyes from him. They would meet in the *asoleadero*. She would stop her sewing and go outside to clear her head or to throw water on her dress so she wouldn't burn up under the blazing sun. There, in the *asoleadero*, they gradually lost their timidity.

FOR MAGDALENA that first day was charged with emotion when, in an unguarded moment and while they were chatting next to the well, Nicolás's hand accidentally brushed against her dress and the soft skin of her thin, strong legs. It was a heat different from the one Milagro's burning sun produced; it was the heat of feathers of white-winged doves coursing right through her dress and spreading across her body. According to some of those books she had been reading in secret, that was the sort of thing that led to sin, but in fact it was the sensation that comes of being a woman, something her mother had foreseen more than once. Suddenly she realized she liked looking at Nicolás, at his strong body. But she didn't stare at him openly. Instead she would wait until he passed by, then she'd look him over from head to toe, including his shoulders and his buttocks. She couldn't comprehend the power of this attraction. To her it was something that went beyond visual pleasure; it had something to do with the mind *and with my blood.*

That was when she began to feel the *mariposas* fluttering in her stomach. And so she would reach under her bed to pull out the books she kept hidden there to see if she could find an answer somewhere.

She recalled her mother's explanations about sin, that it's something that begins as a temptation between a man and a woman. "The fact is that in the real world a girl can get pregnant just by thinking about a man," the mother warned her. Magdalena, for her part, couldn't manage to figure out how it worked, that insertion of the man's vile organ into a woman's body and how from that union could emerge a life separate from their own, her body being invaded by someone else. The whole idea seemed detestable to her. Anyway, she had casual conversations with her mother about what she was reading. After a while she came to give less importance to those little talks because, after all was said and done, the need to get on with life and survive in the real world overshadowed everything else. She had to go out into the street to sell her roses and the clothes they sewed at home when she wasn't spending the rest of her time glued to the sewing machine. So she would take advantage of the little bit of time to herself alone in the privy to carefully review page by page the book she had selected for each particular session. Of special interest to her was the one titled *Health in the Home.* It included depictions of anatomy and nude bodies, and the onset of motherhood.

The mother, for her part, had come to accept the fact that her older daughter was old enough to read the books she kept under her bed, the ones their friend Chele Pintura gave them; he was a local handyman who, from time to time, would drop out of sight from las Angustias. Starting a few years ago, when her daughters were younger, Chele would come by to trim back the wild brush around their property. There was one time when he cut grafts for them from the roses so they could produce even larger and more brilliant flowers. Latina even thought about Chele as a husband for Magdalena one day, *but God told me to forget it, that it was a bad idea.*

The mother had been taking note of Magdalena, how

she was becoming a woman, and consequently she knew the role her daughter was soon to fulfill, the one that nature bound her to. "We women pass through that stage in our lives."

AFTER SO MUCH discussion about Magdalena's feelings, they were no longer able to get to sleep. "I know a woman needs the companionship of a man," the mother tells her. The daughter recounted to Latina her experiences with Nicolás. She told her about that warmth she felt on her skin whenever he came close and how, when he brushed up against her, his touch had a calming effect that dispelled many of the fears she had come to know over the brief span of her life. He made it seem as if the bleak life she led never really existed and that she was still the same little girl she had always been.

Both were young and it was only natural for them to feel that way. "But, you have to resist the temptations of the body so you don't sin. Besides, you're too young to be thinking about men," the mother tells her. And to a certain extent, Latina gave her the idea that all men were evil, only after one thing. And even though they didn't explore the topic any further, Magdalena supposed that that was how things were—all men wanting the same thing when it comes to women. "They have devilish ways and even though you haven't been hurt so far..." the mother warns her. It was another one of those unwritten laws that went back to the time of her grandparents. The daughter got the idea that after a man and woman spent a certain amount of time together the woman no longer needed to regard him as a stranger. In that case there was less risk of doing something wrong. "Don't forget, there's a right time for everything. A time to die and a time to love," the mother tells her. More than anything else, it was because she realized that Nicolás' parents were not going to allow him to go with a girl who had nothing to offer except a poor mother, a little sister, and a dog. "And what do I do in the meantime with these butterflies in my belly?" Magdalena asks. *One day you'll find out you can kill them with your bare hands.* And Latina crosses herself for having had such a thought. For Magdalena, one thing had become clear—that fluttering in her stomach went away whenever she was with Nicolás.

"That's life," the mother says. "But there'll come a time when those butterflies will go away." "How do you know when that time has come?" "Only your heart can tell you that," she tells her. And the mother is afraid of losing her daughter. Magdalena's heart is already speaking to her, secretly calling her, for now it is her turn to fulfill what nature demands. The daughter was never going to be able to kill those butterflies with her own hands because they were already deep inside her, and besides, merely making any reference to her private parts was a sin, not to mention touching them. Moreover, her mother had taught her that a woman's sex was linked to vileness and evil.

ONE DAY they bought a half dozen hens and a rooster, too. It was a good idea. Now they had eggs they could trade at the corner store. They also had a house and a small piece of land they bought from the local government. They were counting on that for their future. Their plot of ground had been communal property at one time and they would be paying it off the rest of their lives. "At least, we have a roof over our heads and a sewing machine. That's enough for now," Latina would say.

Mothers are good when it comes to their daughters, Magdalena thinks. *She managed to send me to school.* As far as Doña Rafaelita was concerned, Magdalena had shown real progress in her studies. She never missed a chance to read the newspaper, which was always two days old by the time it reached Milagro. And in addition to that, the teacher would lend her books. Everything was going along so well until the day her mother had to speak to her. "You'll have to stay home now. I'm going to need your help around here. My fingers ache from all this sewing. Your younger sister will take your place at school," she explains to her. The roles were reversed. Magdalena stays home to do the sewing while the mother goes out to make the rounds of Milagro, selling the clothes she makes, and the younger daughter attends school.

The teacher begged me not to take Magdalena out of school until she finished the primary grades. Latina made the necessary sacrifice so her older daughter could attend classes for two more years. That's how she was able to finish the sixth grade. "A person doesn't need books to get by. If you like to read, that's one thing. But, struggling, surviving—that's another story. You'll have to go to work now. You can't be spending all your time reading those books. There's nothing much worthwhile in them. They're mostly filled with sinful things." "I'll read to you at night, mama. You'll like that." And so it was clear just how much Chele Pintura had influenced Magdalena's interests. *And probably my little sister's too. She was doing real well in school.* They kept the books Chele had given them stored in a box under the bed and no one except Magdalena was allowed to read them.

MAGDALENA WAS my right hand until she met Nicolás. He was the only man she ever had anything to do with in her life since I never let her get too friendly with Chele Pintura. The well had gone dry on the Moreira's lot, so they had to excavate until they found another one. It was during that period that Nicolasito Moreira would come over to visit them. Could they see their way clear to letting him have some water from their well? Magdalena did exactly the opposite of what her mother told her to do: "Men can't be trusted. You can't give them an opportunity." Latina: *So when she finally confessed the truth to me about her and the young boy down the street, I felt like the roof had fallen on me. And then I heard her explanation. She told me about the butterflies in her belly.*

Perhaps Chele would have been better company for her, but it never crossed his mind to speak to Magdalena. It was on account of his drinking. It made him feel cowardly and unsure of himself. *I took to drinking when I was thirteen years old and that was my damnation.* His parents had thrown him out. He was alone on the street. *Or maybe I just decided to leave. I even thought about killing myself, but then I discovered the sea.* When he isn't traveling the world, he returns to his old roosts to do what he knows best—going from house to house in Milagro de la Paz in search of odd jobs. Latina: "You're still young, Chele." But he felt he only had enough strength left in him to help out the people in the Angustias barrio where Latina lived. Maybe that was because their circumstances were different from what he knew. He found a new world for himself. "I've even stopped drinking," he told the mother.

Latina tells him when he doesn't show up for a long time she begins to wonder if he hasn't already fallen back into his old ways. Chele says it's not that at all. In fact he had discovered a world beyond Milagro—the port city of La

Unión where he had no problem at all signing on as a merchant seaman. He could travel the world and be back again, all within seven months. "Before I discovered the world, I didn't feel like living. I had lost all faith," he tells Latina. Now, at least, he wanted to earn his living by the sweat of his brow. "I'm not afraid of any kind of work."

DURING THAT same period packs of *tacuacines* showed up and left the three women with nothing but their rooster and two hens that couldn't lay any more eggs. One night as the mother was getting out of bed she heard the frantic flapping of wings. The hens had been startled by their predators. But, by the time she shone the kerosene lamp in their reddish eyes, the opossums were already out of reach. The summer is a hard time. The problem has to do with the rainy season. The thunderous storms and high winds make it nearly impossible for a person to hear the chickens flapping their wings when nocturnal predators are stalking them.

"That was the danger we faced then. Not like now with these *unknowns* who've started laying waste to the area," the mother says. "*Unknowns.* What are you talking about? There's no such thing," Chele Pintura interrupts. "They murdered my parents at Cerro el Tigre. Men who've banded together to go around stealing and killing. They pretend they're *coyotes* and pigs with the sounds they make." No one had ever seen them. Only their victims and they never lived to tell about it. Chele reassures her: "Don't be afraid. As long as there's hope, there's life, and God too."

That was why the mother welcomed Chele into her home. He restored her faith in men. She would never suspect

Chele of doing any harm to her or her two daughters even though she never stopped reminding them of her daily misgivings: that men were a bunch of shits.

CHELE PINTURA kicked the door open as he came stumbling in. He was carrying a load of two cardboard boxes, one on his shoulder and one on his hip. He heads straight to the kitchen where he knows he'll find Latina. "Chele, what in the world do you have there? You'll get a hernia carrying such heavy stuff." She notices how his legs are wobbling beneath him. Chele tells her the boxes are like a ton of bricks. "But, you're strong, and young too. Tell me, what are you selling?"

"I've brought you some books."

"Oh, dear God. And why would I need books?"

Chele ignores her and sets the boxes down on the floor. "If you only knew what I've got here. You won't be sorry."

"The only one in this house who can read is my older daughter, but she doesn't have time for that, and the younger one has just started school. Besides, I don't think she likes books."

"There's time enough for everything," he tells her.

And then Chele begins breaking the seals on the boxes; they look old and dirty. He has some difficulty opening them, so Latina lends him a hand. "This business of reading is a bunch of crap," she tells him.

Behind his blonde mustache Chele is laughing at her. *You, always with your contrariness.*

"If they're in your way I can keep them here for you, but I can't promise you I won't use them for lighting the fire for our cooking or out back in the *escusado*," Latina says.

When they finished prying open the boxes, a cloud of dust sprang up that made them sneeze. And once they began pulling out the books, there was more dust and they had to sneeze even harder. "They're not in my way," Chele replies. "They're a gift," he says, concentrating on the job at hand.

While he continues talking, the mother begins to examine the books, touching them as if there was something there that might burn her hands. "What good can they do me? Even if they're a gift, I can't accept them. The only use I'd have for them as I said would be here in the kitchen to light the fire for the *fogón* or out in the privy."

"Woman, you're talking gibberish. Can't you see what I'm offering you?"

"What you're offering us is to dump your useless, old books on our floor."

"Whatever you're thinking, just take a look at the interest your little girl has in them," Chele says. He means Crista, the younger daughter, who has come up behind them. The mother reacts: "All right, now. Go on. Get out of here. Don't you see that these books aren't meant for little girls?" And then, turning back to their friend: "Okay, Chele. Let's wait until my daughter Magdalena gets home. She's out, selling her flowers. She's the smart one here and she gets the final word."

Chele smiles—one of the traits that endears him to people. Moreover, physically, he was different from most people in Milagro: light gray eyes, a reddish-white complexion, and blonde hair. That's how he came by his nickname; he was *chele.* He made his living as a handyman, painting posters and signs for the stores in Milagro and doing odd jobs. His was the best quality work around. In fact, Chele Pintura was remarkable. He seemed to extract the colors for his paints directly from nature, as if by magic. But, because he had already painted all the houses and stores in Milagro, there wasn't a lot of work left for him to do. So, then he was forced to begin looking for odd jobs around las Angustias. He looked older than his twenty-five years. Besides his fondness for alcohol, he also liked playing the guitar. "There're five bars in Milagro and I've painted the signs for all of them," he said. More than anything else, it was an outlet, a kind of catharsis for him. All that anyone really knew about him was that he had some schooling beyond the primary grades and that his problems with his parents had caused him to fall into self-destructive ways. "Here, in las Angustias and aboard ship, out there on the oceans, I feel like a different man," he tells Latina.

The mother is thumbing through one of the books: "Ay!" she remarks, shocked at what she sees. "And this leprous woman, what's this supposed to be?" And then, noticing that her younger daughter has come up behind her again: "All right, Crista, stop this sneaking around. Behave yourself. Go on, now. Get out of here. Can't you see these books are for grownups?"

"Latina, these women aren't leprous. It's a book about medicine and it teaches you things about health. It's a treasure. Next you'll be telling me Adam and Eve were lepers because they were naked!"

"Don't go mixing apples and oranges. Look at this," she says, pointing to a page showing nude men and women. "You can't pull the wool over my eyes."

Chele, changing the subject: "One day they found me drowning in a pool of my own bloody vomit and my parents thought I was going to die. My mother cried at my bedside. She sat there for a whole week, praying. My father had a little place on the coast where he grew cotton. He didn't give a damn about me. He said the best cure for me was to go to the Casamata barracks to become a soldier, where they'd make a real man out of me. Not long after that, a blight hit the crops and that was the end of my father's days as a cotton grower. He died later of a heart attack, broke and with no regrets or fanfare. He was a miser, so he must have died a happy man because he didn't leave me a cent, just these books you see here. I don't know why he kept them. I never saw him pick up a single one of them."

"Maybe he read them when he was a young man," the mother offers.

"I don't know. Anyway, I think they'd be wasted on me. Besides I doubt he ever intended for me to have them. That's when I thought about the three of you, especially Magdalena because at least she finished the sixth grade."

"I'd never let the two of them touch these books, not with these sinful pictures. One thing for sure, I won't let my younger one near them."

"But this is the kind of thing you find in medical books. You can't tell me you've never been to a doctor."

"Not even my husband saw me naked. A man and a woman don't have to get undressed to have babies. Maybe my mother and father saw me that way when I was a little girl. That's why I prefer my own medicines, the ones I make from roots and plants. That's what I learned over there in Los Ejidos from Doctor Febles."

The *doctor* from the neighboring town of Quelepa, Luis Febles, used nature's remedies for healing and he had taught Latina his formulas. "He told me, 'Latina, I'm glad that you've come to see me. Look, instead of you having to walk such a distance to come over here, I'm going to teach you how to prepare some remedies you can take in an emergency.'"

"You're lucky, knowing how to look after yourself like that. But, this thing about your husband never having seen you naked, even a priest wouldn't believe that," Chele adds.

"And what would you know what other people do?" she says with a strain of reproof in her voice. "Even if you're my best friend, you still need to show proper respect for your elders." And then, noticing Chele's sheepish smile: "Anyway, we don't need any doctors. I know how to take care of my family. I have my own remedies. I don't need any filthy book to show me how to do that."

"Oh, dear Lord," Chele sighs.

AT THAT precise moment, the younger daughter sneaks in again. She stands over her mother's shoulder, pointing at the book. She opens her eyes wider to get a look at the naked woman whose skin is covered with little red spots. The mother leaps to her feet, threatening to punish her, but Crista quickly retreats.

"Muchachita, as if you haven't been baptized! Scat now if you don't want your eyes to get infected looking at this filth."

And then turning to Chele: "Now you've seen for yourself. How am I supposed to keep these books around? You see what they can lead to." She points to the pages again: "Look. Just look at this pregnant woman with her breasts exposed. It's shameless!"

Chele Pintura realizes the books have captured Latina's attention no matter how much she objects to them. As if she had read his mind, she says with a smile: "It's true, Chele. I've never seen a naked person before, and much less did I ever imagine such things could be found in books. The truth is, the Bible is the only book I know."

Chele, looking triumphant: "If you've read the Bible, then you probably know it's filled with stories about sin: fornication, incest, homosexuality, rape, and other things I can't even mention because I don't want to offend you."

"Don't you dare, Chele! Because then we'd only get in deeper than we already are and that would be the end of our friendship. Besides, as far as the Bible goes, I only know holy stories."

"So, then you admit it. You know what's in them."

"The things you're talking about are probably in that other bible, the one the Protestants read, because I can't imagine such filth in the Catholic bible. What's more, it seems to me the books you've brought us are banned by the law, subversive as they say."

"Subversive? Some of them were banned before, but not now, and this book that has you so scared can be useful. It can teach you how to protect yourself against different kinds of illnesses. You've only seen the photographs of the nude bodies, but it's all about cures. Besides, this isn't the only book in here. I've got books on history and religion, and even some with stories and others with Arabian tales. And don't forget what they say: You shouldn't look a gift horse in the mouth."

"Well, the fact is, I don't need anything from you. And you're a fool for insisting. I already know how to take care of myself. I've got my own medicines. I learned that over in Los Ejidos, near Quelepa. And as far as the other books go, I can't really judge because they're full of writing and I don't know how to read."

Chele, showing his impatience: "I'm doing this for your daughters."

"You're putting me in a bind. For me personally, books don't exist." And then in a resigned tone of voice: "What do I have to offer? Besides not having anything here in the house, Magdalena is the only one who can read. But, she'll never have time for all this. And as for Crista, forget it. She's only started to read and I don't want her learning about this sinful stuff, not even the little things much less the really bad stuff and that's what would happen if she started reading this book. All these dirty pictures."

"One day she'll grow up. Then she'll understand how important books are, and maybe your grandchildren will want to read them, too," Chele tells her.

"And why should you be so interested in giving us these

books? Doña Matilde would probably buy them from you. She always needs extra wrapping paper for the tomatoes and onions down at her store." *It's for Magdalena's sake*, he was about to tell the mother, but he thinks it wiser to keep quiet so he doesn't run out of luck. He wants to keep Latina as a friend and Magdalena as the sweet, untouchable object of his affection.

That's where matters stood when the older daughter got home from school. Chele was explaining to Latina that people who write books aren't bad people, not even dangerous, for that matter. How the contents of a book are viewed all depends on the reader.

"I came here to offer you these books because you're my friends," he explains to the older daughter. "And these sailors, dressed in the colors of the devil, what are they doing?" Magdalena asks. "Well, they were pirates on the high seas, sort of marauders who raided other ships. Some had a wooden peg for a leg, others a hook to replace a hand they lost and others are wearing a black patch over one eye. But the fact is the seafarers in these books were good pirates. They weren't bad. A thief who steals from another thief... You see, the thing is, these pirates only went after stolen goods—gold and jewels others had already taken from their owners." The mother interrupts: "What kind of rules are those?"

"The rules men make," Chele says.

"The rules men make don't interest me," the mother responds.

"It's useless arguing with you, Latina." He explains to the older daughter how valuable the books are. "Just like white gold." But her mother had not looked at anything else except that one book, the one with those photographs of naked men and women.

"God's laws are the only laws that matter to me," she tells Chele emphatically.

IT WAS NOON when Magdalena returned home from school, only to find Chele Pintura negotiating with her mother. They had agreed not to give him too much leeway because you can never trust men. "Chele's a good sort," Latina says. She had always felt kindly toward him. But Magdalena treated him with indifference.

"I don't have any use for the books," he explains to the older daughter. "They were left to me. I know you're going to school, and I thought: Leave them in good hands. Besides, I've already read them." The mother still doesn't trust him completely: "I don't know what good it'll do us having two boxes of old books around the house." But Magdalena feels they should accept Chele Pintura's offer. Crista says nothing. Even though she has already started attending school, she's still too little to have an opinion about something she doesn't understand.

"And what do you want in return?" Magdalena asks.

"I'm just offering you a good deal, but your mother doesn't believe me."

"Aha. Well, then explain it to me," Magdalena insists.

Latina interrupts: "Look. If the truth be told, Chele found these books in the city dump and he's trying to pass them off on us as something his family left him."

"Don't go telling lies, madre."

"I'm not lying and I'm not your *mother*," Latina fires back.

Chele was the only one who knew anything about books. He had lived in other barrios of Milagro where there were schools and other things to do. Moreover, his greatest source of pride was in his claim to being an artist and all because he painted store signs in Milagro. The whole story was really sad because the truth was he had almost been thrown out of his own barrio where the people considered him a vagrant because of his drinking. He would spend the day loitering around las Angustias where his presence was accepted by the women, and he was grateful for that and for the way they treated him, not showing him any prejudice even though he was so different from them, with his blonde hair and light-colored skin, as white as the center of a radish. They were glad to have him do odd jobs for them and they were always polite to him. "When I was eighteen, I sailed to Turkey, and being *chele* and strong and quick to learn, I had no trouble fitting in with the crew." And he tells them that by the time he was twenty he had sailed across the five seas. The mother says there's only one sea just as there's only one sky. Chele smiles. He knows that Latina, despite her contrariness, is a woman with a soft heart.

The only one who doesn't join the discussion is Crista. She stays in the background, like a little kitten—curious, bright, perceptive or maybe a little upset at seeing her mother and older sister giving so much attention to one man. She knows her mother isn't going to put up with her offering any opinion and so she decides to save herself the trouble. Even at her tender age, she can entertain feelings of animosity: *I hate Chele.*

"Let me have a look, Chele," Magdalena says as she begins to rummage around among the books still enveloped in small clouds of dust. "They're dirty enough, but not in bad shape," she says, trying to see if Chele is being honest with them; if he found them in the city dump, they could be contaminated with something and present a danger. "We don't want you giving us anything with germs on it," Magdalena remarks.

"Do you think I got books like these off a trash dump? Anyway, they're in good shape and that's what counts."

"Chele, I'm only joking, but still you ought to know a person can't be too careful about certain things."

"I wouldn't give you something that could hurt you. I wouldn't even do that to my worst enemy. I wouldn't do that to anyone."

"Well, all right. And how much do want for them?" Magdalena wants to know.

The mother intervenes: "It's already been settled. From time to time he'll come over for something to eat, and I told him, as for his coming here, even if it's only for a tortilla with salt, we don't need him bringing us any presents."

"All right. I wish there could be something more, but if that's all you can offer me, I won't quibble over it," Chele answers.

"He'd like us to give him Magda," Crista mutters from the garden where the mother has relegated her so she can't snoop around, sticking her nose into things that don't concern children.

"If I had time to read, I'd be jumping for joy at Chele's offer," says Magdalena. She's excited about the idea of having books in the house even if it meant they'd be hidden away somewhere. One day they'd be of use to someone. But, the only chance she'd ever have to thumb through them and read a few things would be when she was in the privy. She was thinking ahead to some kind of future, one that was yet to be defined. "Let's keep them, mama," she says as she begins to look through them, taking note of certain pages in particular. At school she had been learning how important books were and she was discovering new worlds in their descriptions of things, worlds she wanted to know and be able to explain to her mother and to her little sister.

No one's going to have to explain them to me. I'll read them for myself when I'm grown up, the younger daughter says, muttering to herself. *Magda's not going to belong to Chele or anyone*, and she includes Nicolás too. She has already heard some conversation about him.

"All right," Latina says. "The most we can offer you is a

little bit of *chipilín* soup at noon, or some other scraps of food. That's all we have to eat. If it weren't for frijoles, tortilla, and salt we'd perish. Sometimes the only thing we have in the house is some leftover cheese."

"The truth is, Chele's just a decent sort who wants us to have his books," Magdalena tells her mother in front of the man, but Latina remains wary.

"In this life, there's no such thing as a decent man," Crista shouts from the garden, after having held her tongue so long. Latina reprimands her, telling her to stay outside in the patio, that this business doesn't concern her: "You have too much to say for such a little thing."

"Let her have her say. She's just a child. She's allowed to have her opinion of me," Chele remarks.

"Chele, you don't know anything about children. Don't meddle where it doesn't concern you," Latina tells him.

"Anyway, I always felt you were the only people that should have these books that once belonged to my family."

"We appreciate your kindness, Chele, but you're talking like someone who expects to be dead before long," Latina says with a touch of irony in her voice. A strange feeling comes over her, that someone in her family is going to die soon. She feels a shiver and knocks on wood.

The older sister, whispering: "Mama, don't make jokes like that." And Crista, who has stopped jabbering, has withdrawn to the back of the patio. She is like a cat lying in wait. Her luminous eyes cast daggers at Chele: *There's no such thing as a good man,* she tells herself. *They're all cerotes. Turds.*

"Thank you. So where do you want me to put them?"

Latina calls to Crista to come and help shove the boxes under the bed. She had stayed out of sight and was peering out from behind the patio with the eyes of a furtive hunter. The younger daughter doesn't like the way Chele is looking at Magda. She thinks he's in love with her older sister, but no one is going to snatch her away from them if she can help it.

"Chele, here, and Chele, there." He seemed to be everywhere. Maybe people got that impression because he was the only man in the barrio, except for the soldiers billeted at Casamata, but they didn't seem real. Crista, obedient and without a word, does as her mother tells her. That's the only reason in the world she has for standing so close to Chele. She has a feeling her mother likes the man. Of course, that would mean her mother would have to swallow her own words because, ever since she was a little girl, she had heard her say how men were not to be trusted; weren't they *los seres desconocidos* who disguised themselves as animals in order to steal their hens and dump dead bodies onto the streets of Angustias? *I won't change, not for any man*, she believes with all her heart and all the innocence of an eight-year-old.

Despite everything, they settled on Chele coming around twice a week. "I don't like the idea of having to feed a stranger," Latina says. "A promise is a promise," Magdalena reminds her. Besides, her daughter had been talking a lot about Nicolás Moreira, a neighbor. Having Chele around would be a way of slowing her down, even though Magdalena hardly paid any attention to him. But Crista sees it a different way: "I hate them both." And she said it out loud. The mother scurries outside to the patio, grabs her by her braids, and pulls her toward the kitchen. She orders her to stand in the corner and explains how a child shouldn't repeat what she hears her mother say. "Children should be seen and not heard." And then she raps her on her head twice with her knuckles.

WHAT ELSE could they offer him but their perpetual diet of herbal soup that Latina prepared everyday, thanks to her uncanniness for always finding the right plants? Plants that supply their noonday nourishment, some of which she herself had planted behind the patio.

"You can come by at noon for something to eat. That in exchange for the books," Magda says quietly.

"I don't like the idea of having to cook for a man," the mother says. Latina always fixed the midday meal for Crista and herself while Magda was in school.

When she sees her daughter's mind is made up and it's just a question of Chele coming around twice a week to do some odd jobs for them, she softens. Besides, she feels confident there must be some good reason for Magda's interest in those books. *She knows what she's doing*, she thinks. "Just having books around is a nice thing. A person can get to know the world without leaving home," Magdalena reasons.

"All right. If you're telling me it's the right thing to do, I'm not opposed, but it seems to me those books can lead to all kinds of trouble. They preach heresy and show pictures of naked people," the mother says.

"I'll need to give it more thought if you don't like them," Chele says in a threatening, but playful tone of voice.

"You know I don't know how to read. You can think about it and keep on thinking about it, and it's still all the same to me," Latina retorts.

"Don't talk that way, mama," Magdalena says in a conciliatory tone, so characteristic of her.

"Suppose I take the books to the barber," Chele says, feeling defensive. "I'm sure he'd give me all the free shaves I'd ever need for the rest of my life. But, stupid me, I'm set on them being yours."

"Then why don't you take them to the store on the corner?" insists Latina, knowing full well it is already a *fait accompli* and wanting nothing more than to needle Chele. "At least, Doña Matilde can make use of them as wrapping paper for the vegetables in her store."

"What an awful thing to say, madre. The only thing I want from you in return for the books is your friendship and understanding," Chele says, looking at Magdalena.

"I'm not your *mother*," Latina says, annoyed.

"*Púchica*! For goodness sake! You don't let anyone talk. You're so hardheaded. If I wanted money for them, I'd go over to Casamata and offer them to the comandante. I'm sure he'd buy them from me, but he'd only use them for toilet paper, or better yet he'd probably take me prisoner if he thought they were subversive." He pauses to take a breath. "With you, at least I know they're in good hands."

"Look, Chele, if Magdalena has agreed to it, then let's drop the subject and stop knocking this thing around. It's settled: twice a week you'll have something to eat with us, or whenever you need to come by to clear out whatever's piled up. Just one thing, though; you'll have to take back that filthy book with the pictures of all those naked women."

Chele, looking disappointed: "And just think, the best book of the lot, too!"

Latina, acting as if she doesn't hear him: "And if you want, come by the day after tomorrow. Four can eat as cheaply as three. I'll just add more water to the soup." Crista continues staring at Chele as if he were one of *los seres desconocidos* come to stalk them.

CHELE NEEDED to find work or go hungry. He had no one but himself. But the people of las Angustias always had something to offer him anytime he could take care of some small job for them. The work, once the domain of the men, had been taken over by the women as a part of their routine chores. There was always some kind of odd job for a person like Chele and, whenever he gets a new offer, he knows he's among good people. He got the feeling he could make a life for himself in the Angustias barrio. All the people there were eager enough to listen to him recount his adventures as a young seafarer, his stories about the *camino real*, the royal transport route of the Spanish gold-hoarders—really a jungle trail—through Panama, and his summaries of the books he had read. He would continue helping the people who lived there with whatever it was they needed: getting rid of the weeds that sprang up through the crevices of their patios, giving them advice about certain chemical repellents for the red *zompopo* ants, trimming back the small shrubs that could turn into breeding places for snakes, and making grafts for new rosebushes. It was Chele's skill with roses that really got Magdalena's attention. He could produce a particular variety of red rose which he had named *Meteor* for its fiery red color. And he also produced another variety he called the *Azufre* because of the petal's pale yellow interior.

I respect the people here because they've been good to me and they've accepted me, Chele thinks. And if, indeed, it was true that sprucing up the little plots of land was not a common practice for the people of las Angustias, much less so was it for Chele who could, at least, feel creative when it came to fixing up gardens. He liked seeing the patio free of weeds, even though it was sometimes covered by a blanket of yellow and orange leaves from the *nance* tree, so common to their region. *They accept me for what I am*, he thought. Working for a plate of food and having good friends. What more does a person need who has traveled and known places like Turkey and who reached the top of the map the day he walked down the ship's plank in the port city of Malmø, Sweden? Magda's eyes couldn't see beyond the mountainous green slopes of the Chaparrastique volcano. But Chele was able to describe the landscapes for her: the sea, the snow-capped mountains, the icy lakes and the gilded church domes that looked like they had been coated with honey.

"Those are strange worlds," he had told Magdalena. Worlds that can only exist in the imagination of someone who, after he turned fifteen, had begun to slowly kill himself with drink. Then Chele showed them in one of the books how the earth wasn't only round but beautiful and exotic.

Magdalena, at times bridging the abyss she had created between Chele and herself, approached him to offer a rose for him to take home. But Chele couldn't accept a gift like that. As he explained to the older daughter: "What would they say about me if they saw me—a man walking home with a rose in my hand? The men of Milagro would say I've turned into a woman." But if he lived in las Angustias it would be a different story because there most of the residents were women and they wouldn't think anything of it.

"And why should you care about what other men say?" the mother says, scolding him. "It's your life and you know that men are just a bunch of *cabrones*, anyway. Just stupid pricks. Excuse my language, Chele. I forgot you're a man. Anyway, I don't include you with the others." Then the mother, under her breath to her daughter: "Look, Magdalena, even Chele feels ashamed for how his own kind behave. And he's a man. I've no doubt I'm right when I say they're all a bunch of sons-of-bitches. Nothing but *hijos de puta*." She whispers those last words as if she were afraid God might hear her swearing.

From that day on there were books in the house, but Latina prohibited Crista from even touching them because she was still too young and because of the evil things she could find in them. But the little girl figured it out anyway, how to get hold of them. She kept the book that interested her the most hidden under her pillow and so she could thumb through it without her mother and older sister finding out. That was how she practiced her reading, in addition to what she was learning in school. At any rate, she enjoyed touching the paper, feeling it against her fingers, and she even liked the way the books smelled of old wood because of where they had been stored.

AT TIMES they had nothing to offer Chele, except some hot water flavored with spices and leaves, especially from the end of summer until the beginning of the rainy season. People have to wait until after April for the harvests. The rain storms make those who own land happy; also the poor, but in a different way, because when there are crops that means there'll be plenty of work. But the worker must wait until the corn grows and the coffee beans ripen and the white fruit of the cotton bursts open. "That's when we can sell our clothes to the campesinos and roses to the children for their teachers," Latina says. Just the thought of it is enough to give them hope.

THERE'S NOT much work for Chele and Magda tries to reason with the man: "Chele, you've got to find a way to get back with your own people. Here in las Angustias you'll never find any decent work. No one can afford to pay you. All you'll ever get from us is our asking you for more favors."

"Really, I'm satisfied with the little I have here. I feel useful and I have friends who won't let me go hungry."

"I don't like taking advantage of someone else's hard work," Magda says.

"That's not taking advantage of anything. All we're doing is sharing. You have something, and in exchange I can offer you my time."

"That's enough, Chele. It's not right to talk that way. Work is a sacred thing wherever you find it. A man's labor is always worth something," the mother asserts.

But not long after their agreement, Chele disappeared for six months. No one in las Angustias knew what had become of him. Maybe he had relapsed into his old ways or else he was in a hospital or maybe his remains had ended up on the street, another victim of *los seres desconocidos*, if in fact he wasn't one of them himself.

In that interval of time, the friendship between Magda and Nicolás had grown stronger. He had become the other man in the lives of the three women.

NICOLÁS MOREIRA confesses to her: "My folks don't want me coming over here, and I've told them I'll come here to live anyway even if there are only women." And his parents say "no," that those two women are very strange. He doesn't argue with them. Besides, no one knows much about them. They don't have any dealings with anyone in the barrio, except the woman who owns the store. They would see the mother whenever she left her house, going out to sell her wares. "We refuse to even look at her," they tell him. But it wasn't any different for Latina. She hardly knew Nicolás. He only came by early in the morning when she and the younger daughter were about to leave the house to go out to sell their goods to the campesinos and then they would return at noon. Latina decided to stay out longer, hoping to earn a few *centavos* more. She needed to repair the damage the *tacuacines* had caused. "They're killing off the hens. You can see how it happens, how a mother loses her daughters because she has to go out to put food on the table," Latina says. "You haven't lost me, mama," Magdalena reassures her. The mother, in turn, explains how they're fortunate to still be together. No one can make it alone. Nevertheless, she recognized this was part of life, that link by link, the chain eventually breaks apart until the parents are left without anyone after the children grow up.

Who'll be around to keep me company when I'm old? she wonders She had never known another man after she was widowed and was left with her two daughters.

Magdalena told me about her vomiting. All I could do was hold my peace. I was so angry. But it was also out of respect for her. She was so different from me. I didn't even know how to hold a book between my hands. But my daughter is smart. The worst part was the suffering that comes with being alone. At least, we'll be together. "I don't how you got it into your head to do what you did. You're barely sixteen. To me you're still my little girl." She complains, but accepts it. What's done is done. "So, this is how you reward me for all I've sacrificed."

The Moreira family wanted Nicolás to forget about Magdalena and any commitments he had made to her. "Both of you are too young and all that girl has is a mother who doesn't speak a word to anyone around here. And, what's more, they're poor. Well, so are we, but we're better off than they are."

Nicolás' parents stare at the girl as she walks by, on her way to sell her roses. The father tells his son she's not too bad even if she doesn't have any hips yet. But he had something else in mind. "I'm not going to let my son get mixed up with someone who barely has enough to get by. Besides, they're strange women. No one in Milagro knows anything about them."

They had come down from the Cerro el Tigre volcano in Usulután, when the older one was just a toddler and the younger sister was still nursing. They didn't make friends with anyone on Calle de las Angustias. They're just women struggling to survive, it was rumored. They don't talk; only a formal greeting, that's all: *Good morning. May the Lord be with you.* The people of las Angustias looked on them with pity because they were just two women by themselves and a little girl who was beginning to grow up. They're taking a risk, living here alone. On any given night they could get mauled, they said, talking among themselves. If the *coyotes* didn't get them, then the faceless ones would. Very seldom did they go out together. Mother and daughters lived on a plot of land that lay adjacent to the city dump. A life hidden from the world. "Anyway, no one knows who we are." It was always the mother with her two girls, holding hands, fearful of getting lost. Latina takes a diagonal route across the city to go looking for some cotton fabric in la Cruz, the barrio at the opposite end of las Angustias.

THERE WAS one possible solution for Nicolás: Magdalena could go live with his family, the Moreiras. Just the thought of it was enough to make the mother sick: "It'd be better if he came to live with us." Besides, the daughter didn't want to move out, so she and her mother were in agreement on that much.

Nicolás is young. He's only seventeen. Magdalena's mother went to speak with his parents in an effort to find a solution or reach some agreement, but the Moreiras refused to budge. Their son wasn't going to go live with them under any circumstance. They'd rather see him dead before consenting to that, seeing him stuck in a household where there were only women. The mother tried to reason with them, but the young man's parents came close to throwing her out.

This is what comes of being a woman, she thinks as she goes directly home where her daughters are waiting for her. She doesn't dare tell them the truth about the meeting she had with the parents: "It's no good. They're just a bunch of sons-of-bitches."

That night they all cried together as if each of them

might be the mother of Nicolás' unborn child. "Mama, you didn't cross yourself after saying those bad words," Magdalena tells her. This was one time the mother thought God would forgive her. She had a right to say what she did. "Don't forget Nicolás is going to be the father of my child," the older daughter reminds her.

"Even though you might want to go live with them, Nicolás' folks aren't ever going to accept you as a member of their family," Latina argues. Because Nicolás wasn't of age either. "I already told you I don't want to leave you," Magdalena says. In the end, the older daughter thought they were lucky, the fact that the Moreiras refused to accept her. All the love she needed came from her mother. And while pondering this, she was rubbing her hands over her stomach.

When Magdalena experienced the onset of vomiting, Latina immediately guessed what it was. Her immediate thought was that the moment had finally arrived when her daughter would leave. Hiding herself from Crista and Magdalena, Latina began to weep. Out in the streets, while selling her roses or while the campesinos haggled with her over the prices of her clothes, she couldn't stop crying. It's a wet, rainy day, but Latina thinks the water soaking her dress are the tears falling from her eyes.

Nicolasito intended to come live with them, but that would never work. His parents would disown him for the rest of his life. Latina never liked the idea of taking her neighbors' son away from them even though the daughter tells her, "We wouldn't be taking him away from them." Besides, they lived in the same barrio, hardly a block apart. It wasn't as if they were in some other part of the world. Latina: "I can't get used to the idea of a man living under our roof." It wasn't a question of distance but rather of the relationship between the families. The Moreiras raise pigs, grow bananas and pineapples on a large plot of land adjacent to the one the women live on.

"What good does it do us to be respected if we have so little?" the mother says, trying to console herself. "We only have mangos, *chipilín*, *arbejas* and red peppers." Enough for the three of them. "We have a house. What else do we need?" Crista replies. And despite her tears of anger, she isn't upset about Magdalena perhaps having a baby or about Nicolás' parents being opposed: "Let them go to hell. I'll hate them for as long as I live. Everyone except you, mama, and Crista."

All of life's little stories seem to begin with a mistake. Magdalena: "It's destiny; that's why everything's turned out this way." Latina: "We'll accept this as if each of us was the mother."

"Don't say that, mama. My little sister doesn't know anything about having a baby." And at night: "You have to explain to me how it happened." Bathed in a blue sea of lament.

NICOLÁS CALLS to her from the patio. She stops her work. Until now she had only allowed him to come that far—to haul away the water he needed—and that had been the extent of their relationship except for the few words the boy spoke to her when asking for permission to come onto their property. "You can take the water you need because that's something everyone ought to share," Magdalena tells him.

One day he asks her if she can accompany him to the well. Before, there used to be a bougainvillea or a *veranera* to shade a person's back from the heat while he hauled up the water; now all that's left is a big tree trunk because the termites ate away the rest. The older daughter lets Nicolás take off his shirt and lay it out to dry in the *asoleadero*. He had doused himself with a bucket of water to cool off. The heat's intensity was so strong he felt like he was suffocating. He took the opportunity to wash out his shirt, and it dried in just a few minutes on the furnace-like surface of the stones, stones the women had gathered from the volcano to fashion an *asoleadero* next to their patio. She leaves him standing there and goes back to her sewing. *I look at her and realize I can't take my eyes off her tender shoulders.* She has the shoulders of a woman. Most of the time he hears her singing those sad songs she likes to sing.

"Why don't you ever smile?" he asks her. Because the mother never taught her how, and while she sewed, she would sing songs to help her pass the time, melodies that were for her like the distant chimes of the tower clock that overlooked the marketplace, in *the streets of the Lord* where Latina and Crista sell their clothes to the campesinos. "Noon. That's when they'll be home," she tells him. Noon is the devil's hour, when the sun's vertical fire beats down on Milagro.

Several days go by. Nicolás asks her for a favor: to mend his shirt. "Just a few stitches, please. Here, where the seam is coming apart." Magdalena: "Of course. I'm happy to do it." He stands directly in front of Magda. She doesn't notice how he's staring at her while she concentrates on threading the needle. Her hair has fallen to one side as she pulls the thread with her teeth. She looks up and sees him looking straight at her. She feels like saying something to him. He's acting as if he had never seen her before. *But I don't want to be rude.* Still, she too had never really taken a good look at him either. *I guess we must be about the same age,* she thinks. An age when boys are shyer than girls. *Maybe because we've known the secrets of our body from the time we were little girls.* Women are closer to life's reality. *I better not say anything to him. Fact is it doesn't matter to me one way or the other if he wants to come sniffing around me.* The light from her eyes illuminates the needle on the sewing machine as it advances along the torn seam.

When she's finished sewing the shirt for him, *he asks me*

how much he owes me. I tell him he doesn't owe me anything. "Well, all right. Thanks." *I look at her again. She doesn't realize I'm looking straight at her. I see her fingers curl around the needle so she won't stick herself.* "Well, anyway, I'll bring you some bananas, at least." Magdalena: "You don't have to. I already told you. You don't owe me anything." *Just hearing her speak those words, I'm in love with her more than ever.* Magdalena: *Me too, maybe because this thing I'm feeling comes of a woman's natural curiosity when she feels butterflies stirring in her stomach.*

She had never seen a man's naked torso up close, much less that of someone she felt attracted to. Her urge to say things to him and to touch his chest grew more intense; but she could only do that if he took the first step. No other man had ever gotten so close to her, not to the point of her catching the scent of his sun-drenched body, like the smell of a male goat. Or the scent of a dog when he comes up behind the bitch to sniff her.

I have him try the shirt on. I walk around him, taking the measure of him with my eyes. "If it's too tight, tell me." Nicolás: *I'm not one to bother about small things.* "It's like new." *Then I stay a few minutes longer to talk. Suddenly better than an hour has gone by. I step back with the water and she stops her sewing.* Magdalena: *I hear Mama Moreira shouting to him from the street corner to hurry up because she needs the water. Nicolás tells me he's leaving now.* "All right." Thank goodness, because he was taking up her time and Latina would be angry with her, *if I don't get on with this sewing... We've got to sell our clothes.* Tomorrow is Sunday, a good day for business. The campesinos come into town.

The young man leaves without saying another word. He hoists the large clay pitcher onto his shoulder. A strange feeling comes over her, deep inside: the butterflies are fluttering in her stomach.

WHAT MAGDALENA admires about Nicolás are his eyes and his build. She realizes they're almost the same age. The first time she began to feel the butterflies in her stomach was when he got very close to her. He gave off an odor, something like that of a canine or a frightened deer. He had been sweating profusely, helping his father dig a well. When they finished, he would no longer have an excuse to come by for water, to visit, he tells her. And she gets up the courage to tell him it doesn't matter. "Even if you have a well." He's welcome to come for a visit anytime. Nicolasito knows she's by herself most of the day.

"My mother and little sister don't come home until very late. It helps me to pass the time if I sing out loud while I'm sewing." She tells him her mother had taught her all those songs. Songs of sweet, tragic love. So that months after they finished digging the well, Nicolás comes over to visit the older daughter, using any excuse he can find. He wants to know if she would like some bananas from their trees or if she would let him climb their *nance* tree to get the iguana that's up there. He likes to hunt them. For her part, she feels safer knowing someone else is there with her, at the far end of the patio. "If your mother knew about this, she wouldn't let me come here anymore. But really, we're just secret friends."

One day she showed Nicolás how a person can see the stars inside the well, something she had discovered by pure chance, and really, at first, she thought her eyes were playing tricks on her, because when she looked up at the sky there wasn't a single star. Of course, that was impossible anyway on a sunny morning. But at the bottom of the well there were some coins: small, shiny ones. Both went to take a look and they stood there, close together, looking at them until something began to make them afraid. An unknown universe loomed before them.

In an effort to dispel their fear, they hold hands. A certain feeling comes over them. They would like to stay this way forever, embracing one another, next to the well's stone wall.

Fear is what draws us together, creates in us the need to feel this contact. I feel, and so I know I'm alive.

After a week the mother noticed her daughter was very slow in finishing her work. "You've hardly done any sewing," she remarks. Normally it doesn't matter to Latina if business is slow, but it becomes more urgent with the approaching festival days. That's when the campesinos will be coming down from the Chaparrastique to Milagro.

The mother needs to have enough merchandise. "You're not going to tell me you spend your time sweeping the patio or hauling water from the well," the mother says. If that were so, she wouldn't find the patio carpeted with the yellow and red leaves from the *nance* tree. So, what was she doing during the day? Not sweeping up, obviously. "The pots are practically dry, not even half full. What've you been doing with your time?"

But, Magdalena continued seeing Nicolás. They began to crave each other's constant touch. From there they would progress to a deeper form of communication—through their flesh.

WHENEVER THEY wanted to be together they would meet next to the well. They discovered how easy it was to see the stars glimmering in the water. And each time they drew closer to one another until, at last, he led her to the back of the patio where the hammock was hung and they got in together and began to swing back and forth, wrapped in endless caresses. In the hammock Magdalena's skirt slides up around her hips and falls across her stomach. She manages to straighten it with one hand while with the other one she tries to resist Nicolás, who is on top of her now. Apart from that, it was such a pleasant game they were playing with one another, there in the solitude the patio afforded them.

"We felt like we were the only two people in the world," I told my mother that night. They both held their feelings in check until finally Nicolasito lost all sense of modesty and dared to lift Magdalena's skirt above her stomach. She brushes against the intimate parts of his virile body, secrets unknown to her until now. She becomes aware of certain spasmodic movements and, almost out of curiosity, rests her hand there, causing Nicolasito to grow even bolder until he ventures to place his hands on her stomach, above the waistband of her underpants. He touches her gently with one hand while he caresses her hair in the other. Looking deep into each other's eyes and exchanging their adolescent kisses, each one tasting, exploring the other's mouth, they realize something unusual is bubbling up inside them—she with her butterflies and Nicolasito with those spasms emanating from his groin. It reaches a point where she can't contain herself any longer and she tells him she's going to take off her clothes. He says nothing, but follows her lead. That way there'll be no need to feel ashamed of their nakedness. Right there in the patio, in full sunlight, under the shade of the trees where the hammock is hung, both are impatient, trembling with excitement to know the unknown act, an act impelled by the raging of hot blood. For the first time she can feel the probing touches of Nicolás' hand and of his erect organ. She forgets her mother's warning: *It only takes one time for a man to come inside you for him to spit out his seed and plant a baby in your belly. Just a little bit is all it takes.*

She's afraid, because she knows all too well it doesn't take much for a man to produce another life, but neither can she be absolutely certain of that happening. *And, naturally, I was afraid, but there was something inside me demanding Nicolás' blood and until that moment I didn't know it was white.*

Something frightening, but pleasant. I suppose that's how the first moment of death must feel.

Amidst the gentle swaying of the hammock, the successive waves of emotions, his weight had settled on top of her. She felt swept away and couldn't find the strength at that point to resist what was happening to her. And despite all the difficulties the hammock creates for them, swaying from side to side, Nicolás was trying to enter her, probing her body with his hand. And they felt sure no one would come by. No one would discover them in the solitude of those steamy, hot, ardor-filled days.

It was a child's game. And she sobs in the darkness while the mother caresses her head: "My poor child."

And it went on that way between them every morning until she gradually realized the butterflies in her stomach were fluttering with greater and greater force until she could no longer bear it. She knows she wants Nicolasito inside her, but they have to help each other. They tumble from the hammock, onto the colorful leaves from the *nance*, and roll around together on the ground. So much effort for several days until she finally becomes aware of Nicolás' body enveloped in moistness, the same slippery moistness she felt when he put his tongue inside her mouth. But, now this is different, this slippery wetness inside her other lips, the ones that remain silent, but begin to spread open like a Meteor rose from her garden. The petals seek to bite down, imprison the rigid flesh wriggling in and out amidst the golden streams that flow between her evasive legs. The young man has his arms fastened around the girl's buttocks while at the same time her hands, moving in circular motions, caress his back, trying to hold him so tightly he'll never be able to withdraw from her flesh, *so that he won't be able to spit out his seed and plant a little child inside her,* as her mother says, but instead to keep his hardened flesh inside her, forever asleep. Nicolás has to dig his nails into her flesh so her skin doesn't slip from beneath his fingertips. Her moist legs elude his grasp. The young couple submerged in a river of splendors that ends who knows where. At last, they succeed in finding each other and their flesh joins together. After several days she has the sensation that their bodies are now one, attached to each another, intertwined, consuming each other, pushing against each other, yet remaining at rest inside each other until the stimulus, provoked by their sensations, subsides and he has to leave. *And I, filled with desire, want him to live inside me, cradled in my tireless, carnivorous rose that, with its delicate pulsations, caresses his solid flesh—violent and penetrating. Nicolás, the one who is capable of pushing his way inside me without spoiling the flower of my womanhood.*

He penetrates her now, without any need for her hands to guide him, and his thick honey spills out inside the silence of the empty cathedral that is Magdalena's sex. How can she get up to go inside now where everything started with those butterflies she began to feel? Little by little the sensation of fluttering wings subsides and she can now feel Nicolás' sweet waters flowing inside her body like a warm stream. She doesn't realize there's a child already navigating its way through her virgin blood.

LATINA GRADUALLY drifts off in sleep to the sounds of Crista's breathing. *She lies beside her, in the same little space Magdalena occupied six years ago. Well, it had come true*—the mother's premonition, that is.

Crista and the mother converse under the stone-like weight of the night, but without hearing each other. Time had carried off their memories and their problems had taken flight in a journey that had no return, a journey into oblivion because that was how they wished it.

"Death comes to us but once and we won't die before it's our time," Latina affirms, resigned in her philosophy—the philosophy of a poor, solitary thinker. "The best thing we can do is to sleep. And without the memory of your sister on our minds or anything else," she tells Crista.

Now there were just the three of them, with the little boy sleeping at their side in what used to be Crista's bed. The younger daughter is silent. She makes no reply to her mother's words because tomorrow will be another day just like this one and all the rest. *Memories keep my mother alive. She lives on memories.* But, Latina was satisfied. She had banished life's harshest memory so that her younger daughter might live without grief or pain from the past.

"Leave it to me. I know how to forgive and forget," the mother had told her. She went over to Los Ejidos, near Quelepa, the same little town where Magdalena had died, to visit the only doctor she had any faith in, the same one who could cure so many infirmities, including those of the soul. *If we want to forget.* Well, Doctor Febles could help them.

Tears or just excusing things doesn't solve life's problems. "We'll just keep on erasing everything until God wants us to stop." Still, sometimes at night memories would spring to life in her dreams.

AT NIGHT, Latina and her daughter Crista curl up together under the white sheets. *White shows the most dirt. We may be poor, but we're clean. It's important to me we stay healthy.* Such is Latina's philosophy. Lying side by side in the same bed, mother and daughter talk about different things. They try to remember happier moments, but the sorrows of the past never stop assailing them. Magdalena's image weighs among their memories. However, they had a tacit agreement: they were to bury everything related to the death of the older daughter and all that followed. "It'll be easier for us to get back to normal if we don't talk about certain things," Latina said. But, when they find themselves trapped in that struggle between exhaustion and fear, the struggle between comprehension and blind apathy, they let their guard down and speak the name of their loved one.

They try to induce sleep and, at the same time, to dilute the memory of the past. Oblivion, like a deep well.

Fear grows worse when the night shadows fall, and Crista reasons: "When all is said and done, we're of this world. If the animals are afraid, why shouldn't humans be afraid too?"

They talk on and on, without pause. "You shouldn't chew so much tobacco," Crista tells her mother. Latina is lying in bed, puffing away, but when her cigar finally goes out, she flicks the ashes off and chews what's left. "You know very well I don't swallow the stuff," she tells her.

The daughter has always chided her mother for that habit, but Latina says her *puros* frighten away evil spirits and bad thoughts. "The important thing is to keep the soul alive, not let it wither away," she says. "Let me chew in peace." Next to the bed is the clay bowl Latina uses for her spittoon.

Eyes wide open, eyes of the dead.

Latina completes her thought: "But, this much I know, we're not going to let ourselves become slaves to darkness and fear. The best thing for us to do is to stop thinking so much." Mother and daughter, lost in a hidden world of memories. Latina shouting at the clouds that hang over them: *Even though I have eyes, I don't see a thing.* She maintains her old habit of chatting in bed, before, with Magdalena, now with Crista.

Crista: *Why does she have to talk like that, saying those crazy things? And in the darkness, too?*

A darkness that obliterates everything.

"Maybe I'm just recalling things I should forget," Latina says.

"Stop worrying. We're alive, aren't we? We've been lucky," Crista tells her.

"Of course, you'll outlive me. You're young," the mother tells her, speaking from her heart.

Crista feels Latina's warmth, her encouragement. To her way of thinking, just being able to breathe the air, to have her feet on the ground, to tend the roses she inherited from her sister Magdalena, to watch the trees grow is enough for her to be happy. *That's why God created us, why He put us here.* She pulls the white sheet up over her head. She'd like to remember Magdalena, but it's only a distant name to her, a kind of storm cloud that shrouds her thought. Crista occupies the spot in the bed next to her mother that was once her sister's, but Magdalena's image seems so blurred to her now.

"I never behaved like that," Latina says. She's complaining about her five-year-old grandson Juan Bautista as she draws the last puff on her cigar. "Something must be wrong with him, don't you think?" Crista: "You were probably the same when you were little and we got it from you."

Latina remains silent. In the first place, she disagrees

with her daughter. It seems to her that Crista doesn't share her concerns about the child. On the other hand, she's happy that Crista doesn't take Juan Bautista's stories to heart, the ones about his meetings with Magdalena. It makes Latina feel more confident about bringing up the subject of her older daughter without Crista getting upset. And Crista tries to make amends: "I don't say it to rile you, but it's just you shouldn't pamper him so much."

"He keeps on asking about Magdalena," she tells Crista, referring to the child.

Crista tries to appeal to Latina's sentiments: "Let him be. Let him ask his questions. Anyway, Magda never existed. Wasn't that our agreement?" Latina draws a deep sigh: "Even if that's so, we're never going to forget her." As long as Magda's memory no longer upsets Crista, the mother feels less concerned that the boy may have rekindled some remembrance of her older daughter six years after her death. Taking Doctor Febles' herbal tea produces its desired effect. Their memory of Magdalena lingers only on the surface of a river of thoughts, not down deep. Latina is happy to speak Magdalena's name to her younger daughter. *I never really buried her behind the house. The fact is, she's still with us, always beside me, and when I sleep, I still lie here between my two daughters.* But the truth was she had done everything possible to help Crista erase all the memories buried beneath the surface. *She's young and has to make a life for herself. She shouldn't have anything weighing on her mind.* Without any fragments of an unfortunate life. *We've had our fill of the fears that assail us at night, fears that only heap more suffering on us.* She silently thanks Doctor Febles for his herbal remedy. It helps her forget her sorrows and the memory of her dead daughter.

The house is shrouded in shadows.

In the darkness Crista's eyelids grow heavy. "I remember Magda was my sister because you've told me she was." Her mother listens. And somewhere inside her, there's a hidden pain. Crista was a woman now, her childhood buried behind the house, next to Magdalena. All the rest didn't exist.

Mother and daughter, prisoners inside their four walls.

No one in the house is asleep. Separated by the thin *cancel* partition, Juan Bautista overhears the conversations of the two women. He can see them, their eyes piercing the pitch black darkness—Crista with her eyes open and Latina turning over to spit her tobacco juice into the clay pot next to the bed. That's how they pass the hours. He can even hear the silence. Gradually he drifts off to sleep.

Crista hears her mother snoring and closes her eyes, trying to fall asleep, but she can't. Desperate and perturbed, she grows fearful of the darkness, aware of its dense blackness. Wrapping herself in the sheet, she gets up, careful to not make any sound that will wake her mother. Her agile body, possessing the sinuous movements of a forest creature, is like a thin knife that slices through the darkness, dividing it.

EVERY NIGHT is just like the one before it, the two women rehearsing their day as they lie in bed, trying to get to sleep. Attentive to the wind outside, they re-create the surface of the past. A lake without horizons. An endless, silent flatland. Above all else, the mother tries to protect Crista and wants her to let the little boy alone, leave the *niño* to his own imagination. "No, Magdalena mustn't dwell here any longer. It was God's will. That's how things are," she says. If it weren't for Juan Bautista's strange dreams, there would hardly be any ripples on the slippery surface of their memories. The child had gotten it into his head to speak of Magdalena as if she were with them. "It's all part of the madness we're living."

That's how Crista saw things. As for Latina: "Let him have his illusions. There's no harm in it." There are times when Crista believes Magdalena never really existed. It was an idea Latina had invented so they wouldn't feel they had been forsaken.

"Why's God good to some and not to others?" Crista asks. And the mother tells her: "He doesn't choose which road a person should follow. He just guides us along and then it's up to the person himself to gradually find his own way in life, like the *zompopo* ants that invade the patio." Crista: "Then, what's our purpose in life?"

Perhaps that's a question no one can ever answer. Fatigue crawls over her body. Like cucarachas and lion ants on her skin. "Death's a crock of shit," says Crista. *Life* she must have meant to say. *Sleep. Dreams. You alone give us our only rest,* Latina muses. *Because nothing seems real and yet, at the same time, we're alive.* Living in a prison-world is one thing, but it's another to reach the point of believing life itself is a penitentiary. "We shouldn't feel so threatened by our memories, no matter how bad they are," Latina tells her.

Crista: "One day we'll be like the people from other worlds." Latina crosses herself. She believes it's a great sin not to accept what God gives a person: "To hell with the people from other worlds." She feels like cursing when the moon is full. *The best thing for me to do is sleep.*

Before going to bed, Latina walks over to get the tea she has left brewing over embers that are nearly ashes now. She offers some to Crista. *I take it from her and drink it,* and Latina too. Crista's throat feels constricted by a thirst that still lingers after a day of trekking through the streets of Milagro, selling their roses and their clothes. And Latina, wise in her ways, knows all too well the need to blot out each day so they won't drown in that lake of endless tomorrows. Both of them can face reality with a peace of mind deserved by those who have survived incredible adversity.

Crista's eyes fall shut. *But I can't sleep. I stare at the darkness.* Then wrapped in her white sheet, barely noticeable because of its clean, fresh smell from the noonday sun, she finds herself blindly following the footsteps her memory dictates so she won't stumble in the dark. Bautista is asleep when he hears an anguished cry in the distance. The white sheet spreads itself out at the feet of the child who, at that moment, is dreaming about another visit from his mother.

JUAN BAUTISTA also has his eyes and ears open. He had been listening to some of the conversation between Crista and Latina about death. And in the morning he questions Latina who tells him, "Don't fret. It's just Crista's imagination. When she's worried, she likes to talk to herself. That's how she copes with her bad dreams and the things that scare her. What exactly did you hear, anyway?" the grandmother asks him.

"I heard something about Magdalena, about death," he answers.

"It's nothing. I've already explained to you everything there is to explain." He wanted to know more about his mother. "It's best we don't talk about that," she answers. *It's enough the two of us know what happened. A child his age shouldn't be told certain things*, she tells herself. At five, a child's mind is a fragile thing, like quartz at the bottom of a lake that's filled with dreams.

Juan Bautista heard something else mentioned during those nightly discussions between the mother and daughter, that neither Magdalena nor Nicolás were his parents. He's not always certain if he dreamed it or if he really heard it, but at least his dreams provide him some measure of peace. But still, he's more than ready to take refuge in Latina's words:

"You shouldn't pay any attention to dreams. They lie and create temptations."

Once Bautista is awake, it's a new day, and he stops pestering Latina with questions. The grandmother tells him: "We old people, we'll be dead soon enough, but you've got your whole life ahead of you." Blue like the sky, the day begins to stir itself. The child tells his grandmother: "I love you so much." They embrace. "Crista loves you, too," she tells him. "The problem is she's always working. And when she comes home, she doesn't want to be bothered with anything."

Nevertheless, the child would keep on pestering Latina with questions about things he heard the two of them discussing at night. He says that if Nicolás and Magdalena were his parents, he'd go looking for them and ask them himself. But, that was before his first meeting with Magdalena in the *escusado*, when she told him in no uncertain terms: "I'm *not* your mother, but I'll try to be." And he screamed and ran out. Latina threw herself on top of him, crying in desperation. When she told Crista about it, the daughter tried to convince her she ought to see by now the child wasn't normal. From that moment on, Bautista refused to speak to anyone except Latina. He had willed himself into silence.

"You talk too much about death," Crista tells her mother. And on top of that, Latina had told Juan Bautista the story about the *coyotes* that were circling the house before Magdalena died. "A child is very susceptible to fear," Crista says, reproving her mother. All the while, Latina hasn't stopped weeping. Seeing her mother like that, wrapped in smoke and tears, never letting go of her cigar, Crista begins to comfort her as if she, the daughter, were now the mother: "Don't fret. We've had our bad times, but this is just a small thing." And Crista suggests taking the child over to Los Ejidos. Latina is opposed because Doctor Febles' medicines are for grown-ups, not for innocent children.

Latina: "Doctor Febles' herbal tea is to help us forget the bad thoughts that come to us, but children don't have that problem." Suddenly the memories sweep over her, memories she wants to discard. Ever since the day she had gone to fetch Magdalena's remains, she began living with the fear of losing her other daughter. When Crista turned fourteen, the mother felt she had changed into an adult overnight, transformed from a young dreamer into a woman who was at once rebellious and impatient with the life God had seen fit to give her. *I thought Crista's problems started with her older sister's death. The day we buried Magdalena out back, she turned to me and said, "Mama, I don't want us to live alone here." I had to do something to ease her anguish. It was possible she wouldn't even survive the nine days of the* novenario. *She told me: "Mama, I'll keep trying to do my best, but I have the feeling it won't be long before the* unknowns *come around again and cause us more grief."* Fortunately oblivion took over, and Crista lost all trace of her sister's memory, even what she looked like, and so she was able to go on with her life.

Latina: *I asked her, What do you want us to do? Go back to Usulután?* But that wouldn't have changed anything. Besides, after being away for so many years, no one would even recognize them and they'd still go on being poor and alone. "Here, at least, we've got this house and some day it'll be ours," Latina told her.

Crista: "Maybe if someone else lived with us, things would be different, because without my older sister here, I feel like we're nothing." That was when Latina thought it would be a good idea for them to pay a visit to Doctor Febles. He'd know how to repair their spirit; he'd give them something to soften the memory that assailed them—the memory of a horrendous crime.

However, distant embers still burned, embers they wished to douse, embers that refused to go out.

WHEN JUAN Bautista turned five, they taught him how to haul water from the well. Then one day Latina heard him screaming: "Stars, stars." His cry was drenched with the humidity of the moss and the ferns inside the well. The woman scurries outside: "Why are you shouting into the well like that?" What a scare he gave her! "I want to see the stars," he says. "Whoever told you you can see stars down there?" she asks. "Magdalena," he answers. "Magdalena doesn't exist," Latina replies. "She's my mother." "Muchachito, you must be crazy. I don't know where on earth you get such ideas."

It frightened her the first time she heard Bautista mention the older daughter. *I myself am afraid to speak her name.* "If you say that name again, you're going to die," she tells him.

"What does *to die* mean?"

"It means a person goes to sleep in the ground and never wakes up. Like Plutón or like Magdalena who you just mentioned."

"Or like Nicolás."

"Who's Nicolás?" Latina asks.

If she didn't know, neither would he.

Juan Bautista shrugs, then cranes his neck to look up, hoping he'll see some *azacuanes* overhead. He likes watching the goshawks that roam the sky in aimless flight, piercing through the clouds in lance-like formation.

That was a few days before Magdalena appeared to him in the privy.

Bautista feels good talking to Latina, though he almost never does. She doesn't understand his boredom and hardly ever tries to get close to him. He wanted to be happy, so he had gone to the well to look at the stars inside, but then Latina came at him with that business about *death.* It was a word that jolted him and made his whole body shiver, and so he didn't want to talk about it. An excessive weight for a heart as small as a bird's egg. "It's got to be mentioned because it's a reality." Those were Latina's exact words when talking about death.

Latina makes up her mind not to drop the subject until she can make the boy understand what certain things mean and with that shake loose the fear that clings to him, as if it were crawling inside his very clothes. Bautista, brushing off his shorts: "I like looking at the stars," he says, trying to make Latina understand. Seeing them makes him happy. Latina, reluctantly: "You're not going to die on me on account of some game you like to play. You can see thousands of stars at night. And in just a few more hours they'll all be out." And then she reprimands him. Neither she nor Crista will put up with him hanging face down over the well.

"CRISTA," Bautista calls out softly. He felt her moving around behind him, coming toward him from the wash tub off to one side of the patio. And when he gets no answer, he glances over his shoulder, but sees no one there. He looks again, more carefully now, and realizes that Crista hasn't moved from her spot. She's still bent over the concrete laundry tub, washing clothes. "What's it mean *to die*?" he shouts, picking up a pail of water and emptying it into a clay pot. He repeats his question as he continues pouring.

The younger daughter looks up and glances over at him. He's still standing there naked after his bath, dissolving in the summer's vapors. "I think somebody's calling me, but I don't see anyone," she replies. Bautista, a look of concern etched on his face, persists in calling out to her: "Crista, Crista." Then: "I hear a voice in the distance. Where can it be coming from?" she asks, raising her voice in order to be heard. In the summer mist, the cicadas have flocked together and are flooding the patio with their sound. "The March and April air make people invisible," she says. Bautista leaves the well and comes over to touch her. "Where does so much steam come from?" he asks. "It comes out of the earth; the earth's burning up and evaporating before our very eyes," Crista says, struggling to find the right words. Then she asks, "Who's that touching my hands?"

"Me," Bautista answers, looking worried.

"What a silly pest you are, always pretending to be invisible. Where are you, anyway?" she asks. "Right here," he says, patting her dress. Crista gropes the air with her hands until she finds the child's head. "It'd be better if you'd just disappear once and for all." But, then she regrets what she has just said and continues gesticulating with her hands outstretched: "Oh, here you are. How many times have I told you not to make yourself invisible!" The child examines his body while holding onto Crista. "I'm not invisible," he insists. "Well, then, why can't I see you?" Bautista: "I'm right here." She tells him she still can't see him, but that she'll find him soon enough; all the while she's imitating a blind girl, walking with her arms extended in front of her body. She circles his head with both hands and then touches his hair. "Oh, yes, it's you. There's no doubt about it." She knows him by the feel of his wavy hair, so full of curls. "If you want to talk to me, you've got to stop disappearing like this," she tells him. Bautista answers with a sob. She continues touching his curls. "Well, here you are. But, either I'm blind or you're not a real person." Crista gestures as if to kiss him on his head, but then pulls back. Their little game has become all too real to him and so the child affirms with all his might that he's real; it seems once again he's suddenly afraid, wondering if maybe he really was dead; after all, the only invisible people in this world are dead people; that was the way Latina had explained it to him.

"*To die* means to stop breathing," Latina tells Bautista while scrubbing out his dirty clothes with a bar of brown soap—*jabón de chancho.* That was a hard thing for her to say, but those were the only words she could think of at the time. Then, out of the blue: "Muchachito, why do you wet your bed?" He didn't know why. Maybe he got the urge when he was dreaming.

"What does it mean *to stop breathing*?" he asks his grandmother.

"Well, it means you have a sweet dream that just goes on and on and never ends." Now they're sprucing up the shrubs in the garden, sharing secrets and a little bit of laughter.

Bautista accepts Latina's definitive answer; but it's her presence he wants to feel. He doesn't want to be a little boy from another world.

THE LITTLE GIRL appeared all of a sudden from out of nowhere. She entered the house without knocking and sat down to wait for Latina to hear her story. In a very soft voice, she said she was looking for her *madrina* and that this was the house they told her to go to, but Latina hadn't the least idea who her godmother might be. "You should have knocked before coming in. You were lucky the dog didn't bite you." The little girl tells her she's not afraid of dogs, that if a person's not afraid of them, they won't bite. Those were the last days Juan Bautista went around the house naked.

Latina and Crista made him put on his shorts. A little girl was going to be living with them and he couldn't go around showing his *cositas*. Naked on account of the heat in Milagro de la Paz, heat and wind that come down from the Chaparrastique before the sun sets behind the volcano. The day is aflame with heat and the air reverberates. By evening, the winds out of the sky and those from Honduras and the Caribbean cool things down.

That's why he went around like that, *the way God brought me into the world*, while he plays in the patio. *At night, Latina wipes me down with cotton swabs soaked in alcohol so I won't soil the white sheets with my sweat and dirt.* And also to initiate their journey into the night with dignity and cleanliness, a journey Latina considered a brief but treacherous crossing. A fleeting adventure every twenty-four hours for the family that now included Lluvia—the little girl from the Chaparrastique who had suddenly appeared at their door, looking for her godmother.

Latina: *My guardian angels sent her to me. Now I have*

someone to talk to besides the stones and the trees and the little garrobos on our place. Because it's only been in the past year that Juan Bautista stopped talking and that's been hard on me. There's no talking with him. God knows I've tried.

"Muchachito, what ails you that you can't even tell me the names of things?"

In the beginning, he could barely pronounce the r and s sounds. But that day he came running out of the privy and shouting, he stopped talking altogether. The only letters he could pronounce with any clarity were the vowels. The younger daughter tells Latina to leave him alone: "That's how *cipotes* his age act." *And so I let him be.* In any event, they took him to Doctor Febles over there at Los Ejidos and he told them the problem would stop once he lost his baby teeth. "Still, it's so strange how he just stopped talking one day," he said. Latina: "Maybe he'll show more interest in talking again now that we have Lluvia with us." Crista: "Leave him alone, mama. Just the way he stopped talking, that's the way he'll find his tongue again." Latina wasn't too worried about it; at least she could understand his gestures. Besides, she didn't have that much to say to him anyway; she just talked to the stones and the chickens they had out back. But now she would have the little girl to talk to.

"You'll have to put some clothes on, just like everybody else now that you're growing up," she told him. "Every day that goes by, you're turning into an *hombrecito* right before our eyes." Yes, their own little man.

WHENEVER HE insisted on running through the patio naked, Crista would stop him, warning him that if he didn't listen to them he'd disappear from the face of the earth. "No one will be able to see you. You'll stop existing," she said. *That means I'll be all alone,* he thought. "If no one can see you, it'll be like being buried alive out back, next to Magdalena and Plutón," Crista warns him. But he's willing to risk it, especially when the heat becomes so unbearable for him. *I'll take my clothes off and then I'll be invisible. I don't know how Latina does it, going around in her fustanes and her long dresses that reach her ankles even if she doesn't wear anything underneath. I know because when I go out back with her to the toilet, she lifts up her skirts and just does it. I like to hear the tinkling sound her pee makes when it comes out.* All in all, she's meticulous about how she dresses. Even at home, she wears an ankle-length slip that's white and fresh, and a pleated skirt, almost always with dark colored patterns against a white background. *Our sheets are white, too; so bright they sparkle.* They shine in the dark. Latina always has the clean, fresh smell of soap about her.

His instincts remind him he can't keep going around the house naked now that there's a little girl living with them. *Ever since she came here, I've stopped taking off my pants except when I get into bed. She looks so sweet when she's sleeping, like the angels that surround the Salvadorcito del Mundo. That's a painting that tells my grandmother things even though I don't know what they say to each other. I don't want Crista to see me naked either. Not even Latina, and she's my grandmother. At home, it's only in front of our dog Chocolate that I don't feel embarrassed.*

The last time he forgot to put his pants on was when he tried speaking to Crista, making gestures and voicing words he could barely articulate; she didn't pay any attention to him. He told her he thought he heard a voice, but he didn't know where it was coming from, and after a while she just ignored his babbling even when he would be screaming and asserting his presence: "I'm right here! I'm real."

He's next to Crista now, touching her, wanting to be sure she's there, and once he feels the pleasant weave of her cotton dress, *I'm not scared anymore.*

I've always been afraid of becoming invisible because then I'd disappear, just like Magdalena. I never knew her, but I hear her name mentioned sometimes in the evenings when Latina and Crista are talking.

More recently—at night—he has begun to get the feeling that someone has been getting into bed with him to keep him company: *after Latina has put the candles out and I'm already fast asleep, or half dead with fatigue.* He hears the shadow walking toward him. *It comes over to my bed and gets in with me.* He thought he saw a white sheet walking toward him, but he wasn't afraid. He thought it was a woman, even though Latina had told him that the guardian angels who keep watch over little children were either of the masculine sort or just the neutral kind. "Still, I wouldn't like the idea of some man sleeping with you, even if he's a guardian angel," she says.

My grandmother tells me it's a sin for a man and a woman to sleep together. I have certain reasons for not telling her about that nighttime visitor. She'll think I'm evil. "And what about a man sleeping with a man?" he asks, thinking about the angel. Latina reacts sharply: "Niño, you see how God made us and you can still ask me something like that!" It was heresy.

On several occasions he overheard the conversations between his grandmother and his sister at bedtime. "The only problem with keeping secrets is that our conscience starts to bother us," the grandmother says. Before going to bed, they drink their herbal tea, a special brew of dried herbal leaves: *bella de noche* petals, crushed mint, and anise seeds. Latina sighs: "Thank God for Doctor Febles being so good and giving me the recipe so we don't have to go way over to Los Ejidos every month." *I hear them talking, Crista and Latina. They sleep in the same bed. I'm not afraid.* Knowing Lluvia was sleeping next to him in the hammock that once belonged to Magdalena.

When the tremor came I thought it was the end of the world because you think the ground is going to open up and that it'll be over for us. Latina told me: "We're going to sleep outside under the trees tonight." The volcano wasn't going to kill us, but outside we ran the risk of a snakebite. A string of garlic around our neck protects us against poisonous things. They spread their *petates* on top of a cushion of *nance* leaves. *That was the first time we ever spent a whole week sleeping outside in the patio. I remember that. I was getting used to the stars. But we wouldn't always be running for cover from the volcano, Latina said: "If it wants to bombard us, then let it, but it just wants to throw a scare into us, that's all."*

He hears footsteps, the footsteps of the dead. Perhaps they're the same ones that get dumped onto Calle de las Angustias. Dead people in pain. So long as they don't have a piece of land to be buried on, a Mass to be said for them or someone to claim them, the dead will be damned, purging their suffering in the flames of hell. *The only thing I like about sleeping outside in the patio is that I'm closer to the three of them and that makes me feel safe. Latina, Crista and Lluvia. Sometimes they put me in the middle if winds are coming down from the mountain or out of the north so I won't be frozen stiff by morning.*

After several days, now that the fear of the tremors had passed, they go back inside; the grandmother, Crista, and Lluvia work hard to make up for the lost time. *My sister is at the sewing machine while Latina makes buttonholes and sews the buttons on. And in the back, in the shadows, I'm stretched out in my bed. Lluvia washes the utensils we use at mealtime and cleans out the ashes from the fogón so the evil spirits won't find a place to hide themselves. What I like best about being under a roof is that I can listen to the owls flapping their wings in the dark.* Hoot, hoot, hoot. And now, after spending several days out there in the patio, he can still hear the sound of the leaves and the wind.

He finds pleasure in some of the nocturnal images and in lying down together on their *petates* with the ground underneath them. "What I like about being out in the patio is seeing the sparkling lights that shine down from the sky," Latina says. Because inside the house, the night is pitch black.

At home, there're four of us, counting the dog. I sleep on a cot while my grandmother and my sister sleep in a big rickety bed made of agave. Lluvia sleeps nearby in a hammock. It too is made of *agave.*

I never stop thinking about Magdalena even though Crista says it was because of her I stopped talking. Latina tells me Magdalena's my mother, that if I disagree with her on account of the voices I heard one night, then "that's your business; she's your mother and the fact is she's dead, and the dead are invisible and that's why they aren't real people." *And I feel happy having a mother who's invisible like me.* "The good thing Magdalena left us is that she carried off the *unknowns* with her," Latina says. "Ever since then they've stopped bothering us. They're afraid of the soldiers who patrol the streets all hours of the night," she affirms. "I think what happened was that they felt satisfied with Magdalena's death," Crista says. Latina: "There's no reason to think such a thing." Crista: "Yes, there is. The *unknowns* want a death in every family. That way each is a flesh and blood lesson to teach the rest of us." Latina: "If we've done nothing wrong, we've nothing to pay for." Crista, in a sleepy voice: "Original sin...that's what we pay for."

I like listening to them talk at night. Lluvia, she's the only one who falls asleep peacefully as soon as she gets into bed.

THE ROOM is divided by a cloth panel decorated with colorful pictures cut from magazines. Latina tucks the little boy in every night, and with complete solemnity, silently tells him, *adiós*. She tells Crista: "You never know, with this terrible volcano."

Generally, after dinner, Crista stays up late to do her sewing, and her mother keeps her company. As soon as the daughter shows the first signs of weariness, Latina gets up from her chair and, holding one of the candles, goes over to shake the bed, checking between the sheets for scorpions or a snake. "You really pamper Juan Bautista," Crista says in a tone of protest, "but you don't bother with Lluvia." Latina: "It's not the same thing. Lluvia already has the instincts of a young woman; she can take care of herself just like us." Crista: "Do you mean to say that men are different?"

"No," Latina says, defending herself. "It's just that Juan Bautista is still a helpless little *cipote*." Then she goes over to check on the child, to ask him if he's asleep. He says he is. "How do you know?" the grandmother asks.

Because I can hear you over there, I hear myself telling her.

THE WALLS of the house are blackened with the soot from the *fogón*, which in the past occupied a corner of the main room, next to the bedroom the two women share. Since the older daughter died, the work had been piling up for them until all hours of the night. There was no way for them to wash down the walls much less patch up the holes and crevices that provided hiding places for crickets and spiders, and sometimes scorpions. A few days before she died, the older daughter had decided to take the *fogón* outside to the patio, behind the house. "This smoke and soot are going to kill us." But the walls stayed black. "Some day I'll plaster over them and give them a coat of whitewash." Magdalena was never able to do that.

Once Latina reaches her bed, she extinguishes the candle she has in one hand. She gets in, dead with fatigue, but still holding onto her cigar; the *puro* spends more time between her fingers than it does in her mouth. Wide awake, she's puffing away on it, waiting for Crista and Lluvia to come to bed.

Chas, chas. The sound of tobacco being chewed.

Exhaustion leaves the two women tense, unable to sleep; they're worn out. They'd rather talk. "We can't eat unless we work," Latina says. There's frequent complaining. Either out of self-pity or to give themselves the strength to go on. Their constant laments have nothing to do with any lack of desire or resolve on their part; they're always ready to begin the next day's work.

"You chew too much tobacco," the daughter reiterates. The grandmother, defending herself: "It's good for the bugs." And *chas, chas.* "It helps me chase the mosquitoes away."

THEN I FELT the shadow walking slowly towards me, or something so soft it seemed to be flying. I pulled the sheet up over my head because I didn't want to see anything. I wanted to let out a scream to wake the women, but I thought I was dreaming.

But dreams aren't reality.

He clung to his blanket. He had heard something breathing. Slowly he slipped out from under the sheet, but all he could see was what seemed to be an immense tunnel of blackness inside the house. His eyes were riveted on a patch of white that stood out in the dark.

I wrap myself in my blanket, squeezing it with my hands

that are more like cat's paws at this moment. And by the time I've said the Prayer of the Anima Sola for the fourth time, I drift off to sleep. I hear it getting into bed next to me.

Afterwards the white shadow retreats to the sound of fluttering wings or a chant. Like Castilian doves. A sharp cooing sound they make when they're frightened and take flight. Or like those chants he had heard once when they visited the hospital chapel in Milagro. The darkness ushers him inside a prison.

And after saying the "Prayer of the Lost Soul" so many times, I can now see her the way she appears in the paintings: naked and tied to the tree; her wavy hair and angel face, and those luminous eyes.

She was the only woman he had ever seen naked and it happened when he went to the festival in Milagro one time with Latina and Crista; there she was, displayed inside a framed picture on the walls of several booths; it was typical of all the festivals. He liked looking at the *Anima Sola*, but it also aroused his fear because there she was, being consumed by the flames of hell.

The white shadow bent down, wanting to listen to something inside my chest. Maybe to know what my heart was saying. It's a dream I have every night. When day comes I've forgotten everything. I don't say anything about it to anyone. The idea of it getting so close to me scares me because I talk in my sleep.

He didn't want the shadow to know his intimate secrets.

AFTER THE DEATH of the older daughter and the *novenario*, they became more aware than ever of their loneliness and how it would fill their nights and their conversation: "We need someone, but we've no one else now;

we're alone," Crista complains. Hardly ten days had gone by since Magdalena's death. "We can't go on like this," she repeats. And she wasn't given to complaining; it wasn't in her nature.

Crista: *Ever since I can remember, we've been accustomed to our little chats at night; it's a way for us to feel less lonely.*

"Sometimes I ask myself why you make up so many stories, or who could have told you all those things; you scare me," the daughter says, addressing her mother. Her eyes—wide open in the dark—reveal the measure of her fear. "We've got to forget everything that's happened," she tells her mother.

"My tears haven't dried yet, but we can't carry this burden with us the rest of our lives," Latina answers, even though her mother's heart was telling her otherwise.

We keep talking as long as we can't fall asleep. "This place exists because of a miracle of Providence; if it weren't so, we'd already be dead," Latina says. That was how the town got its name. *Ten eruptions every hundred years is too much for Milagro de la Paz.* "The volcano heaped great rivers of lava on us, but the molten rock separated and divided itself in two before it reached Angustias." In its wake it left a half-moon of destruction and through the years it gradually transformed itself into a complete circle: an entire sea of black rock. "But, at least the volcano didn't touch our homes; it respects them," the mother says, finishing her thought.

"I don't know where you get such ideas," the daughter insists.

"Still, I'm scared, what with the tremors we've had of late," Latina admits.

"Mama, the volcano doesn't want to hurt us. We shouldn't worry ourselves over something that hasn't happened yet. I'm sure it doesn't hate us."

"We have to pray so the Chaparrastique won't bury us alive," the mother says.

"If we've run out of luck, the Chaparrastique's going to bombard us no matter what, and if your prayers work, we'll be saved."

"I know that's how it is, but that doesn't mean I can stop worrying. We're not made of stone," Latina says.

"I'm sure these new rumblings won't turn into an eruption," Crista says.

However, the fear was always there—like a centipede, lying in wait for the two women who talk about their loneliness and the small world they share together. "We're alone, but that's life." It's a patience amassed after five hundred years of Christian indoctrination. Their religious conviction was their last hope. "We need to hold on to our faith to have peace of mind," the mother tells her daughter. Even if they had a man in the house, "we'd still be afraid to go outside to sleep in the patio." "Men are braver than women," Crista says. The latest tremors brought strong rumblings, like bombs. "Bautista, he's our *hombrecito*," Latina tells her. They feared a holocaust. "The best thing for us to do is to go outside and let God's will be done," Latina says, trying to bolster their courage. "Bautista's useless to us. He's not a man yet," Crista replies. The following night they decided to go out to the patio. Both women were thinking the same thing. "Where are we going to get a man, then? Of the two we know, Nicolás is dead." And Chele had gone off to sail around the world again on one of his many journeys across unknown seas.

SHE TURNS over, her back now to her daughter, and feels around on the floor for the clay bowl she spits her tobacco juice into; it seems the only way for her to induce sleep is to chew tobacco. She extinguishes the cigar with her tongue; then biting off the end, she begins chewing until she feels a drowsiness that culminates in a sweet repose.

"One day you'll be a woman and you'll have the man that God chooses for you," Latina tells her daughter. They begin to fall asleep under the chirping sounds of the crickets and the silent gnawing of the termites. "Men go off and leave their women," Latina tells her. Crista: "I don't think I'll ever live with a man." Latina muses: "It's too soon to talk about things like that, especially at your age. You're not even fourteen yet; and it's just as well that you not worry about any of this, because before you know it, someone can come along that you like."

Crista normally lies on her side, with her hands under one cheek for a pillow. A posture of complete repose. But, this time she's lying on her back, with her hands behind her neck because she knows that she's not going to fall asleep any time soon. "And what man could that be, mama? Have you ever known one you thought was any good?" the daughter asks. "Maybe, your grandfather, but there's always some fly in the ointment. One time he kept my mother tied to a tree for two nights," Latina answers. The mother and daughter lie very still, like two sisters from another world. "It's probably better for you not to think about men. You're still too young to understand any of this. Besides, I'd be left here all alone," Latina says. The room creaks with restlessness and the night. "Anyway, he untied her two days later after he made her swear she'd never be unfaithful to him." Of course, she would never be unfaithful to him, but the grandfather wanted to hear her swear her love for him; that was his idea of being romantic.

IN TIME we became friends with the man who had given Magdalena his books. It hadn't been so long ago that he came by to offer his condolences and ask us to forgive him for not having come to the funeral or the wake. "It was only today I found out she was dead and so I came right over as soon as I heard. She hadn't offended me in any way. What happened was that I shipped out again." He had sailed to Japan. "I never stopped thinking about you." *He said if he could be useful to us, he'd start helping out again with some of the little things around here just like before.* "Chele, it's best we don't talk about Magdalena. We want to forget the past. It's barely three weeks since she died. Her blood's still fresh on my clothes and my hands." He says goodbye, but returns the next day while Crista is out, making her rounds of Milagro. He realized the younger daughter was never going to forgive him for having offered Magdalena his friendship.

"If you want to erase Magdalena from your minds, then I've got to respect your wishes," he tells them. Then he changes the subject and recounts to Latina his adventures on the seas. "I imagine it's just like flying across a liquid sky and a salty one at that," Latina comments. "It's different," he says, although he had never flown. Latina had the idea that the sea was thick, maybe something like oil. "That's how boats stay afloat," she adds. Chele explains: "The sky is made of a liquid crystal that's weightless." Planes can fly because of an unwritten law called "inertia"; it's as if the plane is tied to a string and its motors keep it in orbit; the string provides the velocity and the earth is the hand that keeps it up there. And that's all there is to it.

"That Chele's a smart one," Latina remarks to Crista at night.

"He's a *farsante*," the younger daughter says, calling him a liar. She had read the books that had belonged to Chele. "It's obvious he's never read them." Latina tells her she shouldn't talk that way about him: "He must have some regard for us or else he wouldn't have come back here to las Angustias, not a man like that who knows the world, to return to this trash heap, a place where buzzards circle overhead, over corpses no one can identify." Crista tells her emphatically: "All men are pigs, mama. You've told me so yourself and I think you're right." Latina: "But you're too young to be talking that way. You don't have any experience to be able to say that with so much certainty." Crista: "I agree, but there's something about him I don't like." Latina, seeming concerned: "You shouldn't talk like that. There's no reason for it, not from a little girl like you who's so pretty and studies so hard." She's referring to Crista's passion for reading and her interest in the books that were once Magdalena's. "I don't know why we left Magda alone in the house like that. It was as if you just wanted to hand her over to Nicolás," Crista says. Latina protests: "You're talking nonsense. I never wanted to hand my daughter's life over to anybody." She's disturbed by the anger that's been festering inside Crista; she was too good a girl for that, and, at the same time, she excuses her: "When all's said and done, we're just two women living alone; we're on our own and we don't owe anything to anybody."

"In any event, Chele isn't from our world," Latina says, resigned in her feelings. It mattered little to her what Crista said about him. And pondering these things, she falls into a deep sleep, with her cheek resting on both hands.

Chele wasn't the only man people saw around las Angustias; there were also the soldiers from the Casamata barracks, but they had nothing to do with the civilians other than their visits to the corner grocery store. Even though some said the soldiers were good, nevertheless, given their training, they still behaved like soldiers, carrying out orders that sometimes made people afraid of them. They were the "guardians" who maintained order and defended the people in the barrio against the criminals, but corpses were always showing up on Calle de las Angustias.

"Why did Magdalena get a tickling sensation in her belly when she thought about men?" Crista asks. Latina can't give her an answer at that precise moment. She had just finished chewing her tobacco and is already half asleep. *My mind is too clouded to answer her.* The daughter's voice seems distant, muddled with other sounds: faint echoes from the wings of nocturnal birds; the crickets and the termites immersed in the silence of the night. In the darkness, sounds of hungry animals sniffing in every corner.

She'd explain it to Crista some other time, that when a girl begins to feel the fluttering of butterflies in her belly, it's nature announcing itself. The memory of her own adolescence comes to mind: *I also experienced the same feeling when I was young, before I had you and Magdalena, and you'll feel the same flutterings, too, when your time comes.* She's only talking to herself, because she's got to get some rest. Tomorrow's another day, just like this one. Crista insists: "I feel them sometimes. Ever since I turned thirteen." Latina can't rid herself of certain thoughts: *One day she'll go off with a man even though now she says she hates them.* She was sure of one thing: *Nothing's going to come between us.* And she begins to snore. *I like hearing her when she snores,* the daughter muses as she strokes the mother's body. She recalls Magdalena's death and Nicolás' apparent suicide two days later; they found the boy hanging from the pulley of their well. However, she had recognized the smell of gunpowder on him and wounds similar to those they found on her older sister who had been murdered over in Los Ejidos, the very same place they used to go whenever they were sick, to see Doctor Febles, the local *curandero* who cured people's ills with his *aguas azules.* He had recommended a mixture of certain herbs they could make themselves *that we were to take half an hour before going to bed. It was supposed to erase all our bad memories.* After three trips to see the *doctor,* he told them: "Look here. You're poor. There's no need for you to wear yourselves out walking all this distance if you can grow these plants on your own property."

Latina: *Thanks to that medicine we were able to forget our mistakes, our regrets, our sorrow.* Their recurring dream.

LATINA TEACHES Juan Bautista and Lluvia how to bundle up and leave only a little hole for their nose and eyes. This lessens their fears so they can sleep more peacefully. "That way you won't smother," she tells them.

Everybody is resting, their eyes closed.

Except the little boy: half-asleep, half-awake, half-dead. He, too, had difficulty falling asleep; perhaps a family trait. *Why should I be afraid of the dark?*

Bautista tells himself stories to ease his fears. *Why do people disappear?* He had heard it on several occasions when the two women would be talking at night about Magdalena and sometimes about Nicolás. Even Lluvia said her own parents disappeared.

After that first night, when he saw the white shadow in the room, he grew accustomed to the creaky sound of those footsteps that seemed to leave imprints in the air. The outline of a white sheet approaches in silence and a living body gets into bed next to him. *Death's coming to get me.* The shadow lies down at his feet. It remained very quiet, motionless; it didn't move a muscle. Sometimes it caressed his feet, which were always clean even though he went around barefoot; it was Latina who took the most pains in making sure everything was kept clean, using cotton swabs soaked in alcohol to do the job. The caressing sensation on his toes was so feathery he confused it with his fear of the night, although he was sure the footsteps and the shadowy form were real, because once he had even grabbed hold of the warm feet next to him. *I'm sleepy.* Meanwhile the shadowy figure was kissing the tips of his toes. Fear is a natural thing, but his fears diminished with Lluvia's arrival; and she slept in the hammock close to his bed. Now he wouldn't feel so alone, and if the shadow, wrapped in a white sheet, should come and get into bed next to him, it wasn't going to frighten him anymore.

We're all going to die.

"You talk in your sleep at night," Latina tells Juan Bautista, emphasizing her words, reproaching him for imaginary sins. He thought he was only talking to himself, but the grandmother doesn't miss a thing. When he talks, he barely moves his lips. And if he shouts that he's hungry, he holds it inside so only his stomach, which screeches when he's hungry, will hear him. "I'm hungry." Latina: "Child, you're always hungry. You must have a tapeworm inside you." Crista: "You have to give him coconut milk if you want to kill the parasites in his belly."

But he feels happy just knowing that Latina looks after him at night and that Lluvia sleeps next to his bed. He never knew his parents, but he didn't miss not having any either; Latina was all he needed. A person doesn't miss what he doesn't know. And Crista only ignored him. "Maybe if Bautista had been a girl instead, the situation could have been different." That's what he heard at night when the two women were discussing things. And even Lluvia had nothing to say to him. *She doesn't understand me either.*

"I've *never* gotten into your bed. You're imagining things," Latina tells him.

"Then, the white shadow must be a dream. Or a guardian angel," he tells his grandmother.

"You can't see guardian angels. They don't caress your feet either. That's why I say it's all your imagination. And, God knows, I wouldn't touch your feet," Latina tells him.

"Then who's been coming to sleep next to me?" he asks. In the distance the child sees Crista approaching.

"You're always thinking bad thoughts. You'd be better off not mentioning that white shadow again because all you'll do is attract more bad thoughts," Crista says, looking down at his frail body which has begun to quiver. She has adopted an air of indifference when speaking to him, acting as if he didn't exist. "Why couldn't he have been a girl?" she asks her mother.

He manages to fall asleep to the music of the distant stars and the sounds that please him. Hoot-hoot. An owl screeches as it goes fluttering by.

THE MOTHER remembers when there were only three of them at home, she and her two daughters. There were tremors in Milagro de la Paz then, but they didn't cause any damage.

"The best thing for us to do is to stay inside. That way we won't be taking any risks," I tell Magdalena. "The animals are more of a danger than the Chaparrastique." Especially the coyote-dogs and snakes that the rumblings stirred up. *Only Plutón stayed out on the patio those nights. Two days later, when I was still without sleep, I heard Plutón whining. In the morning, the dog didn't come to greet us when we opened the door. We began calling him.* "Maybe he fell into the well." *But, we would have smelled a foul odor if that were so. Besides, the dog wasn't that stupid.* "He probably went out to the street," she remembers Magdalena saying. "At noon we saw some *zopilotes* circling above the garbage on the adjoining lot." Latina hopped over the stone fence to see where the buzzards were circling and she spotted a coffee-colored bundle on the ground. *I climb the mountain of trash and I see the dog's body on the other side. Maybe he had fallen asleep there, but suddenly there was a buzzard swooping down toward him.* She ran to frighten it off and found herself standing next to Plutón. He was still alive. *I began to shout to my two daughters. I tell them that Plutón's dying. I dragged him from the mound of garbage back to the house. I lift my leg over the stone fence with the dog in my arms. Both my daughters are trembling with anger and worry.*

"Who could have done such a horrible thing?" *I ask them. But, they don't answer me; they're crying. Magdalena's looking him over.* He has several bites on his neck. She inserts her fingers into the wounds. "His neck looks like a sieve, but he's alive," *she tells me. He's got more than ten puncture wounds, all teeth marks. The three of us are standing there; all we can do is hold each other tight.* Latina says the coyote-dogs have come back. They did this. "I smell a strange odor," Crista remarks. *We're holding each other so tight we aren't able to let go. Then I tell them:* "We can't save him!" *And I'm trying to save my strength for what's ahead of us.* "I smell gunpowder," Latina confirms. *We try to save him, shoving pieces of panela between his teeth in case it was poisoning. Surely miracles must exist.* "Poison doesn't make holes," Magdalena says. Latina asserts what she believed was true from the beginning: "It was those men who disguise themselves as animals and wail at night."

We buried him next to the privy, out there behind the patio. We made a stone cross and set it on top of the ground. Magdalena and Crista come up to me to console me: "Don't worry. We'll get another dog." *It wasn't about the dog. It was then I knew these faceless murderers had discovered our house and all that stood between them and us were the soldiers from Casamata.*

HE WAS the family dog. Someone had made those wounds around his neck. Latina treated him with pieces of *panela* they placed between his teeth and salted lime juice just in case he had been poisoned; it was an antidote for *vidrio molido*: an old method people used for getting rid of a dog that annoyed them or that they considered dangerous. Finely ground glass hidden in some food the dog could get hold of.

"Will he die?" the younger daughter asks, bending over until she feels the dog's dying breath on her face.

"*Hijos de puta*," was the mother's hoarse reply. Those sons-of-bitches.

"He used to put a scare into people," the older daughter says. She tried to rationalize what had happened and lessen her mother's bitterness.

"He used to bark, but he never bit anyone," Crista-child remarks. She's still a child.

But Magdalena began to examine the animal more closely. "His heart's still beating." That was when she realized there were wounds on his neck. He hadn't been poisoned as they thought at first. It couldn't have been the *coyotes* because they devour their victims. Then it must have been *los seres desconocidos* who did this.

Who's going to look after us now? But, Latina holds her tongue; whenever confronted by a difficult situation, she knows when to speak and when to keep silent. The younger daughter has stretched out on the ground and is watching her mother and sister as they try to save the animal's life. The dog opens his eyes one last time. They all know it. The mother, as she almost always does, is quick to say what's on her mind.

"I think we need a man around here."

"But, you know that men are evil," Crista replies.

"Not all of them," Magdalena says defensively. She has been seeing Nicolás and is going to have his baby.

"Who's going to sleep with me? Who's going to keep us company now that Plutón's dead?" the younger daughter asks. Especially on those dark nights, stained by black clouds and the menace of coming storms, when their only light is the lightning that flashes across the sky.

Plutón used to lie at the foot of Crista's bed; now he was no longer with them. "I'm scared," Crista says. It was as if the house were blanketed with fear. And the mother explains to her that they'll just have to get accustomed to sleeping alone.

"We'll look out for each other," Latina says.

"Nicolás can stay with us," Magdalena says, but no one hears her or wants to hear her.

"The wounds on Plutón's neck look like bullet holes, but they're really fang marks," Latina comments.

"Are we going to feed him to the buzzards?" Magdalena asks.

"No. We'll bury him behind the patio and put up a cross. We'll use the stones from the volcano," the mother replies.

"I'm scared. The cross is only for *cristianos*," the younger daughter says.

"What's the difference between Plutón and a human being?" the mother mumbles, talking more to herself than to her daughter; she doesn't want to get into a discussion with her at this time. "Even an animal deserves a Christian burial. I don't know why we shouldn't do the same for Plutón," the mother says.

Crista-child smiles at her mother's way of putting things.

Latina: *There've been only a few times I've ever seen Crista laugh, like that time I was complaining about almost never being able to see anything that was going on down the street anymore because our fence of piña in front had grown so high, but then suddenly as I was peering through the thicket I see Chele approaching, and I say,* "Look, it's Chele. He's got no shame! *Peeing* right there, out in the open, in the middle of the street."

"Mama," *my daughter said, scolding me,* "there are certain things a person shouldn't be watching even if you happen to see it." *We joked about it afterwards.* "How is it that men like to pee the first spot they come to, anyway?" Crista asks. "That's how they mark their territory," Latina says. "They wear the pants."

"They're nothing but *exhibitionists,*" Crista-child asserts.

"I'd hate to see Plutón being carried off by *zopilotes,*" Latina insists, thinking that dead dogs end up getting deposited on Calle de las Angustias. She helps Magda open Plutón's mouth so they can insert some *panela* between his teeth. That could revive him if he had been poisoned. Maybe she could even save him from his wounds.

The truth was that it was Magda's dog and she had gotten into some arguments with several neighbors who had accused the animal of being overly aggressive, even fierce. "Look, we're all decent people here. There's no need for him to be barking at us that way and scaring us." Starting at sunup, as soon as Plutón would hear the soldiers trotting about in the early morning hours, he would begin barking.

The whole thing has my mother on edge. She thinks a person who could kill somebody's dog is capable of killing people too. "God help us!" the mother cries. But maybe not this time. "Someone had it in for him," she affirms.

People were scared of Plutón because he was so big and barked a lot. He even went after other animals that came onto our property, but what Magda says is true: he never hurt anyone. And almost never left the house except to go out to greet Magdalena when she came home at the end of the day. He would only go after someone who would come in without knocking first. "He left us the same way he came to us," Latina remarks. The dog had shown up at their door one day, having wandered over from the municipal dump when he was a pup and still needed to be nursed. Someone had thrown him on top of the trash to get rid of him. *And we fed him rice water to trick him because we didn't have any milk. And the poor thing managed to survive.*

And I grew even more fond of him when I saw he had learned to carry Magdalena's basket in his mouth. "Whoever killed him probably did it so he could get into the house."

"They kill just because they have nothing better to do," Magdalena says, speaking softly, as if someone might overhear her.

My older daughter is worried. "No one's going to break in," I *tell her. Still, all of us were thinking the same thing, that Plutón's death was a bad omen.*

And at that moment, a swirling wind came down from the volcano, a *remolino* so strong that it lifted the dog straight up into the air. "It's the devil himself," the mother mutters, making the sign of the cross.

Then we went over to the garbage dump to look for him and there he was. "This is all we needed, to be left more alone than before," Magda says, seeing Plutón lying there dead.

"I loved him, but we shouldn't be taking it so hard," Crista-child says as they finish burying the animal. *I stand there looking at them, at my two daughters; a dark feeling comes over me, and I begin to cry.* Standing in the doorway that faces the patio, she watches them come toward her, both of them beautiful, both of them looking so sad.

A YEAR LATER my older daughter died; we tried to erase Magdalena's memory, hoping to lift the awful weight from us. She was carrying Nicolás Moreira's child. We had even accepted the idea that he'd spend some time with us.

Magdalena had gone to the nearby town of Los Ejidos to sell their clothes and didn't come home that day. The next morning, the mother went out to look for her. When she reached the town, they told her they had found a dead girl in the *corredor* of a house in Quelepa; there were wounds, deep punctures around her neck that formed a collar of blood. Unfortunately, it had grown late and darkness had overtaken her, so she couldn't make her way back to Milagro de la Paz. A family had offered her a place to sleep—the *corredor* alongside their house that opened onto the patio. In the morning, they realized she had not awakened.

No one dared touch her. She was still there, lying on the floor—dead for several hours. The mother, seated on the back of an ox-drawn cart, carried her home, wrapped in a blanket; she held her in her arms as if she were still alive, their legs dangling over the edge of the cart. She had recognized the familiar smell of gunpowder and she filled up with anger and pain. *It was those men who disguise themselves as animals.*

She caresses her daughter's swollen stomach. She detects the slight palpitations of an infant who probably wasn't going to survive.

Six years after Magdalena's death, Lluvia came along. The little girl walks past the barrier that hangs at the entrance to the *corredor*; a curtain of delicate, green vines, laced with colorful, wild flowers. From the kitchen area in back, the *vieja* heard the stranger approaching and calls out to her in a calm tone of voice: "Muchachita, stay where you are. Don't move. Sit down. Easy. Don't let him see you're afraid." From where she was standing, the old woman had also seen the dog—the new one, Chocolate—always on the alert in the presence of anything that moved. The little girl sat down as if she hadn't heard the grandmother's warning. Latina walks up to the dog, now standing at the little girl's side; the stranger whispers something: "I'm not afraid of dogs." And to prove it, she touches his head and the animal lies down at her feet. The woman tells her, "You've performed a miracle, because this one doesn't abide any strangers here. What's your name?"

The woman begins to query her, but gets few answers. The little girl strokes her dress, carefully smoothing it out as if it were something fragile—like glass—and might break.

"Don't ever enter a house without knocking first," Latina, says, reprimanding her, still not believing the dog's docility. But the little girl, a bit nervous, is stroking his head.

"I saw the door was open," she says after a few seconds. Latina: "A person must always ask first before entering a house."

The child says that she did call out, but maybe "you didn't hear me." Her words echo in the solitary surroundings, float from tree to tree, glide on streams of air in the sky.

She had said, "*Buenas tardes, le dé Dios.*" Good afternoon, God be with you. But no one answered her. She had seen Latina at the end of the *corredor*, blowing on the hot embers in the *fogón*, and a dog at the other end of the patio, and in the distance, a little boy who was hiding behind some bushes.

Latina, calmer now, asks her again: "What's your name?" She looks her over, notices her *tombilla*, the little, round bamboo basket, off to the side; she's wearing pigskin sandals and, attached to the top of her head, a stream of colorful ribbons flowing down behind her back, a *chongo* that also ties her pair of braids together.

"My name's Lluvia." Then she falls silent and waits; she knows she'll have to answer the questions put to her by the woman sooner or later. From the back of the patio, she hears a little boy's voice calling the dog. Latina thinks: *I must be going crazy; it's as if Magdalena has come back from a long journey, only she's come back as a little girl.*

"I've come down from the volcano," the little girl says, looking up into the branches of the trees that surround the patio. With her eyes, she peels back the leaves which block her view of the Chaparrastique, the volcano that overlooks the valley of Milagro de la Paz.

"Such a pretty name you have, even though I've never heard it before," Latina says, repeating her name. *Rain.* Once more Lluvia turns her gaze toward the Chaparrastique and the woman follows the girl's anxious eyes.

"You came all the way down from up there?" "*Díos mío,*" she says to herself in disbelief. Latina's eyes turn to scan the view of the volcano's gaping mouth which looks as if it's swallowing the blue sky. "I always wanted to go up there and touch the clouds with my hands," says Latina, as if the volcano belonged to Lluvia. She wants the little girl to feel good and believes it's only right to make her welcome. Payment for this brief moment of happiness the child has brought her, to be reminded after all these years of what Magdalena looked like. After so many relentless, somber nights, her older daughter's face had become a faded image in her memory, like a sweet dream whose details cannot later be recalled; even though she had never forgotten her, of course. With her fingers, Lluvia points upward, between the branches of the trees, out toward what looks like an immense wave. The volcano looming over them with its truncated cone, capped by white, billowy clouds that look like a sombrero. *Gateway to hell.* The little girl, in response to what Latina said about touching the clouds: "You can only see them from far away, but when you get close, you can't see them; they become invisible."

"That's an odd name; it's almost like being called *Agua.*" She can't fathom the idea of someone being named Lluvia. Calling someone *Rain.* "Well, I've learned something new even though it doesn't make much difference to me, but I always thought the clouds were real." Lluvia explains to her that they're real, but "what I mean is that you can't see them up there; it's only when you're down here."

"Oh, that's a different story then," Latina remarks, sighing quietly. *What am I doing, discussing clouds with a little girl, a stranger?* she asks herself. *Only my heart knows why.* The truth exists even when it's hidden.

"And you, what's your name?" Lluvia bravely asks her while turning around to glance at the little boy at the rear of the patio.

"I'm Latina and the *cipote* is Juan Bautista, my grandson," she replies.

LLUVIA EXPLAINS: her parents had told her if she ever went to Milagro de la Paz it wouldn't be hard to do; you just follow the road in a straight line all the way down; keep your sights on the houses in the distance until you reach the cemetery at the entrance to the valley and that's Milagro de la Paz. The city was founded on May 8th, 1530 by don Luis de Moscoso, on the shore of the Texcuco River, the same place where the soldiers go to wash their clothes and bathe in the nude. Not much has changed since that time.

A few more answers follow: Lluvia had arrived early in the morning after coming down from the highest part of the volcano. To a child of nine, ten hours in a slow, ox-drawn cart can seem like an eternity. "I told the man to let me off here." That she would know where to find her godmother. "And the farmer told me, *Be careful walking these lonely streets, especially Calle de las Angustias.*" She saw the graves in the cemetery and the long barbed-wire fence and *amate* trees that provided shade for the dead. She was a little frightened, nothing more. She didn't know there were so many dead people in Milagro. Latina tells her it's nothing for her to worry about; they dump most of the dead bodies here and then the buzzards carry them off in their beaks up into the clouds that ring the volcano. From there it was easy to reach this house which fit the directions she remembered.

From way up there on the Chaparrastique, she could always see Milagro de la Paz—the little red houses which only now she realized appeared to be that color because of the roof tiles. After following the road off to the right, she reached the dusty street her parents had described. Calle de las Angustias. Dead dogs; buzzards swooping over the remains. At times, the body of some *cristiano*, a sight which should only be viewed by family. No one's allowed to touch a corpse. The law forbids it. First, the authorities or someone in charge has to come, but they take their time or maybe they just never show up at all.

Lluvia explains to Latina that once a girl leaves home it's very hard to go back; the parents act as if she's gone off forever, never to return. "It's for our own good." And the parents understood that: there's work to be found in the city; a person has a chance for a better life.

A family offers something money can't buy, but Latina can't find the words. She wishes she could talk about affection or love. Lluvia realizes that death is a constant topic with Latina. And even though she's just a little girl, she had just experienced the same emotions herself. It was as if the subject of death had become the mortar which was to unite an old woman with a little girl who was a stranger, and create a sense of trust between them. Tragedy is the common ground. Milagro is *tragedy. Tragedia de la Paz* would be more like it.

"There was no future for me on the mountain," Lluvia tells her. Lately there had been many fires and the coffee trees were no longer producing very much. The families had grown tired of working and not having anything to show for it. Moreover, there had been tremors. And wild dogs, frightened by the fires, would come scurrying out of their caves in packs and ravage the fields.

Latina asks her a question she had been putting off for a while: "And what happened to your mother and father?"

"They're dead."

"What do you mean, they're dead?" Latina is nervous and would rather not insist too much. Besides, she doesn't even know her.

"When a girl leaves home, her parents no longer matter to her because they stay behind; they cease to exist." And nobody in the family knows what will become of her.

How is that you speak with the tongue of an old woman? Latina wonders. "It's pure chance you happened to come to my house because I'm not your godmother."

Lluvia, humbly: "It was the only address I had."

That was lucky for me, Latina tells herself.

Only a few minutes ago her little world of Angustias seemed so insignificant to her. Magdalena's death had distorted her sense of time and numbed her memory, or rather her pain; she wonders if it would have been better for her not to have erased the memory of her older daughter these past six years. And she's thinking about the past and comparing it to the happiness she feels at this moment in the presence of the little girl who has come to awaken a renewed hope in her.

There's a long silence from Latina. She, too, had come to Milagro de la Paz under similar circumstances, looking for a new life; but, all that was years ago. Lluvia's arrival reminded her of that period in her life. Now she viewed her as the very person she had wished for, someone to fill her emptiness—and provide her some companionship. Since Magdalena's death, she had been so wretched, unable to reconcile herself to the fact that she was going to be without a family one day. It was God's will and it was out of her hands. Her blurred memory of Magdalena had tormented her these past six years.

"I also lived near a volcano, El Tigre, before coming to Milagro. It's so long ago that it seems like a dream. Next we went to Usulután and finally we came here to live." She feels better, talking to someone, not just the stones in the *asoleadero* or the *garrobos*—little iguanas—and the trees. "We came here on a train, my two daughters and I; Magda was four and Crista was an infant.

She decides to change the subject, taking advantage of the fact that Lluvia hasn't stopped watching the bushes out back, beyond the *corredor*; some are in bloom while others are withered, their little branches laid bare by the summer heat or the red *zompopo* ants. But it's really the little boy that has captured her attention.

"I never thought much of the idea of having a rose garden, but I feel like Magdalena's here with me; as for me, I'd rather plant things like chile peppers, *ruda*, *hierbabuena*, and *arbejas*." She preferred the peppers and herbs because she always associated flowers with death.

"They're pretty," Lluvia says, looking at the roses.

She had guessed that Lluvia liked flowers. "You could

help us tend them." But she's distracted by the little boy and continues observing him.

"Why does he stare at me so much?" she asks.

Latina: "He likes to run around naked; he probably feels embarrassed now that we have a visitor; no one ever visits us." Latina is thinking about how lonely Lluvia must feel. "And do you remember when you were baptized?" she asks the little girl. She says she doesn't. "No doubt you don't even remember what your godmother looks like." Well, no. This is only the second time she has ever been in Milagro; the first time was when she was an infant, when they brought her to the church to be baptized. The little boy decides to go off to play next to the privy even though he would like to be able to say something to the new girl. "The dog's name is Chocolate," Latina says. She tells her the rose garden is Magdalena's legacy.

LLUVIA, for her part, had grown calmer when she saw that she had come to the home of someone who spoke to her in such a reassuring way.

"I'm sure you've got the wrong house, because no one has ever asked me to be present at a baptism," Latina says, lighting up her first cigar of the day. She pulls up a stool. "I'm a mother, but not a godmother." And then she smoothes out her dress to make herself more comfortable; she's glad to be talking to a real person for a change and not just to the stones of the *asoleadero* or to El Salvadorcito del Mundo—the Christ Child—her favorite saint who stood before her in a framed picture that hung on her wall.

Lluvia asks her for some water. She's perspiring after her trip down from the Chaparrastique and the sweat is dripping into her big eyes.

"I completely forgot," Latina says, distracted by Lluvia's

chongo. "I meant to offer you some; in this heat a person can get so thirsty he can't stop drinking."

The little girl's colorful ribbons flutter with a dazzling brilliance and once again capture Latina's attention, or else her eyes are playing tricks on her; perhaps it's her age. "Have you had anything to eat today?" she asks. Lluvia says nothing. The grandmother asks her if something's wrong and then waves the cigar in front of her eyes to see if she has perhaps fallen asleep. The *chongo* seems to continue fluttering in the air.

Lluvia remains silent, unable to put her feelings into words; to be more exact, she was thinking about how hungry she was. It had been more than six hours since she had anything to eat. *I'm so hungry. How in the world am I going to find something to eat?* she wonders. But, she said nothing. Suddenly, as if awakened out of a dream, she casts a glance at Latina's floral-patterned dress; she seems bathed in its colors. Lluvia likes admiring the mother's bright cotton dress of liquid crystal.

Latina comes over with some water and asks again, "Are you hungry?" She likes having Lluvia there. She sees herself in the child; also, her older daughter Magdalena, many years before when they left Usulután and came to Milagro. *Suddenly I feel so alone*, she thinks.

"I had a little bit to eat on the way," the child tells the mother. She feels bashful about taking anything from Latina. She looks at the little boy and at the dog who have come closer to stand at the edge of the *corredor.*

"Sometimes he locks himself in the *escusado* and no one can get him to come out," Latina says, referring to her grandson. "Now he's taken to going around with the dog all the time."

"I'm hungry, too," he says. He had been hiding behind the rose bushes; he spends almost all his time with Chocolate. Lluvia merely nods her head as she takes the water from Latina. A brief pause. "I've never seen roses," she says. "Honeysuckle, yes, because lots of them grow on the volcano." She hurriedly drinks the water, gulping it down. And Latina tells her not to be shy about it because she can see it in the child's eyes that she hasn't had anything to eat since she left home. Lluvia tells her that she ate some flowers as she walked along Calle de las Angustias, those that grow on the stone fences. "I ate some begonias." Like little drops of blood. "How awful," Latina says.

The dog begins barking nervously. "My *chongo* is scaring him," says Lluvia, not paying attention to the dog's threats. The colorful ribbons keeps fluttering.

"Those flowers, the ones that grow on fences, don't satisfy a person's hunger," she tells the child. But, if she wasn't hungry, that was her business. Latina feels intrigued by the *cipota*'s presence. The thought that immediately consumes her: *I need Lluvia; I need her here with me, but I don't know if the soldiers from Casamata will figure out that someone else is living here, someone who doesn't belong to our family.* She needed to have another person she could talk to; she couldn't just go on talking to the trees and the stones in the *asoleadero*. Communicating with her grandson was very hard now that he had practically stopped talking; only through a laborious effort of using a sign language they could both understand were they able to communicate with each other. I'd rather talk to the iguanas and the stones in the *asoleadero*. Sometimes she even talked to the birds and the volcano.

Lluvia's colorful *chongo* gives the grandmother the impression it has several sets of wings. She makes no remark about it though, because several months ago she realized her eyes were no longer the same as before. Dazzled by the fluttering ribbons, Latina says, "They look like butterflies."

THE MOTHER makes the sign of the cross just thinking that her eyes might be failing her; the fact is she had never seen a *chongo* like that before, one so colorful and waving about as if it had wings. Latina plays innocent: "What do you have in that *tombilla*?" she asks, referring to Lluvia's little, basket that contained all her worldly possessions.

Latina keeps on talking. "If it were up to me and you don't have any other place to go, you can stay here, but first I'll have to talk to Crista." She glances again at the child's hair, at the fluttering *chongo* above her braids, and she begins to feel uneasy. The woman's nervous movements betray her ambivalence. Islands of silence. Then she confesses to the little girl: "I'm not the only one who makes decisions here; my daughter's involved, too." Because she's taking a risk to have someone living in the house who isn't a member of the family, for reasons having to do with age-old disputes between the military comandante and the residents. "A long time ago these were community properties."

"We just have this little *solar* of ours. We'll be paying for it the rest of our lives." But, they had come anyway, dragging their misgivings along with them. "They won't leave us in peace because they don't trust us, even though I pay what I owe every month for my right to live here." She makes the sign of the cross and changes the subject. "What do you have in there?" she asks, pointing to the girl's bamboo *tombilla*.

"Some clothes and a red coral necklace." She says it with the confidence of one who has finally found her real home. "It'll be dark in a couple of hours," the little girl remarks, breaking the stillness of a deep sea of thoughts.

Latina looks at the sky, the only timepiece she knows. "It's almost four o'clock and Crista's not home yet." She walks over to the *fogón* where there are always some scraps of food, even if it's just a piece of tortilla. "Well, I'll bet you're hungry."

"Who's Crista?"

For the time being, Latina can't leave the house to go around asking about the girl's godmother, but come morning she'll be able to help her, and her daughter would be home soon, but not until then were they going to discuss whether or not "you can spend the night here." Although she was wondering how anyone could deny shelter to a little girl like Lluvia. Where could they send her if it was going to be dark soon? And not knowing anyone.

"Crista's my younger daughter. She usually comes home a little after four o'clock. Maybe she went off to buy something in La Cruz; that's a barrio on the other side of las Angustias." Lluvia, ingenuous: "And your older daughter? Where's she?" Latina tells her she's out back, behind the patio.

"Yes, I'm hungry. Thank you," she says, stretching out her hand as Latina offers her a little bit of tortilla. The grandmother had buttered it with some lard and added a pinch of salt.

"She's dead," Latina sighs, without explaining anything to the little girl.

The child eats hurriedly. The grandmother can't take her eyes from her. "Slow down. No one's going to take your tortilla away from you."

Juan Bautista inches his way over, drawn closer by Lluvia or by the smell of the tortillas; he wants to say something, either about someone or about his dog, but they won't understand him. He knew his mother wasn't living. He always thought Magdalena was his mother until he heard something to the contrary. "You know very well Magdalena and Nicolás aren't his parents," he heard Latina telling Crista. Then that must mean that he, just like Lluvia, had come out of the blue. From nowhere. The child then heard Latina sobbing. And the next thing he knew was that Magda appeared to him in the *escusado* and confirmed what he had heard. *That's why I stopped talking.*

Latina is the only one who can understand him. As for Crista, the situation is even more difficult even though they don't even look at each other, one avoiding the other. Latina would like to share a thought with Juan Bautista that has just come to her: *How nice it would be if Lluvia could stay with them.*

Lluvia could, at least, keep me company. Until I die. And she saw a difficult and endless road ahead. *Maybe if we told people she's my daughter.* Resurrected from the dead. She thinks that it's the one way to get around the military governor's order that prohibits an outsider from residing in the Angustias barrio.

Latina has grown bored talking to the walls, walls full of spider and scorpion nests. *Of course, I've got Juan Bautista.* But her only communication with him is completely elementary. The little girl, on the other hand, is something so new, a surprise, an opportunity for her to feel less alone in the world. A few hours later she told Crista: "The other choice probably is for her not to leave the house, to stay shut up inside"

As for the dog, Chocolate, having him around was really more of a bother than anything else. If Latina showed him any kindness at all, it was only because he was a replacement for their cherished Plutón who had belonged to the deceased daughter.

"I'm going to the door to see if Crista's coming." Latina ignores her grandson's babbling. "I don't see her yet." The anxiety over sharing Lluvia's providential presence with her younger daughter has her on edge.

"YOU'LL MEET Crista soon; she'll be here any minute now. She's the one who'll decide," Latina tells the little girl. Lluvia, submissively: "I understand."

Latina: *Why do dogs look like people? The only problem is they can't talk.*

Crista normally gets home around four in the afternoon.

"God help me, you're such a *cipota*, and walking around these streets all by yourself." And she told her to have a seat on Bautista's little stool, motioning toward it with her finger. Or was it with her Honduran cigar? "It's unbelievable to me how a little thing like you could make that trip all alone down from the volcano."

Latina returns to the *fogón* at the far end of the *corredor*.

"Lord, help me! Walking all by yourself along Calle de las Angustias." Latina positions herself under the protective tin roof covering that extends the length of the *corredor*; she's going to toast a tortilla with a sprinkling of lard on the wood-burning *fogón*. "It's not much, but it quiets the stomach for a while."

And Lluvia remained seated, wrapped in a cloud of silence, interrupted by the buzzing of mosquitoes in the early evening air and by Chocolate's hungry growls.

"Crista's late; she's almost always home by four." Her tardiness exasperates Latina.

Juan Bautista is playing with the dog. The *cipote* approaches and Latina strokes his curly hair, her fingers reaching down to his scalp. The child withdraws without uttering a word, not even a babbling.

Lluvia stays perfectly still, thinking she's in another world, different from the home she knew on the volcano.

Juan Bautista: *I'm looking at her, sitting there on my taburetito,* his little stool with the calf-leather seat. She seems lost, but after eating the tortilla, she felt more at home.

Crista should be home by four o'clock; she had gone to the La Cruz barrio to buy some cotton cloth. "It's after four," Latina says, reading the position of the sun, near the mouth of the Chaparrastique.

"Will Crista let me stay?" Lluvia asks.

Latina looks uncertain, the same as Bautista, and even Chocolate, suddenly fallen silent after sniffing Lluvia.

"I don't know, muchachita; in any case, it's also up to me whether or not you can stay."

The younger daughter would be home soon now that the sun was beginning to disappear behind the Chaparrastique's crater.

"I'm afraid to tell you yes, because the comandante controls everything around here," Latina says, thinking about the soldiers from Casamata who could show up unexpectedly and discover they have a stranger living with them; but, she felt sure Crista would let her stay, although she'd raise some objections first because that's the way she is. She always wants an explanation.

"We shouldn't have to be afraid of the soldiers; we're in our own house."

"MY NAME is Lluvia."

"That's a pretty name," Latina says, at a loss for words. *But it gives me a strange feeling. I don't-know-what.* The luminous fluttering in Lluvia's hair makes her nervous, but she goes about her business without making anything of it.

Latina asks the usual, obligatory questions about the little girl's family and where her parents are. "I'm still thirsty."

"Wait," Latina tells her, getting more water. "Thank you." They like talking to one another.

And she repeats that she came down from the Chaparrastique to look for her godmother. In the early morning hours she had been making her descent down the side of the volcano.

"You know, I had a daughter who died and ever since then no one has come around to question us about anything. Maybe that's what they call luck." She'd rather not go on discussing that chapter in her life. It had been several years since she mentioned Magdalena by name.

"What's your godmother's name?" she asks her.

She's not sure. She fiddles with her braids, parting them with her fingers to scratch her head. "It's on the tip of my tongue. I don't remember."

Latina's eyes are riveted on the shimmering colors of the two living, breathing butterflies. Finally she dares to ask: "And who put those *mariposas* in your hair?"

Crista, who had come home earlier, interrupts, saying it wasn't possible to forget someone's name from one day to the next. "And what did they tell you? How were you supposed to find your *madrina*?"

"They told me it'd be very easy. They said everybody in Milagro de la Paz knows Calle de las Angustias." She'd know the street when she saw the buzzards flying overhead, scavenging for dead dogs and sometimes the corpses of poor folk. "I just followed the *zopilotes*. They led me here." She pauses.

"Ever since I was little, I've been accustomed to having these butterflies in my hair." Latina, spellbound, smiles admiringly.

The child sheds some light on how it had been explained to her, how to find her way down to the cemetery in Milagro, then follow the paved road for a kilometer on the right until she entered the city at Calle de las Angustias, the third street over. Some time ago her parents had told her: "You'll know it when you get there because the street's filled with dust and there'll be buzzards flying overhead."

All the roads at this end of Milagro de la Paz are dusty, except the one that runs for almost two kilometers from the railroad station to the cemetery, then continues on, joining all the countries of the Americas.

They told her that her godmother lived two blocks beyond where Calle de las Angustias comes out; at any rate, she could ask for her once she got there.

"According to that, that's where we live, but no one here is your godmother. It can't be Crista and it can't be me you're looking for because we'd know it if it were so."

"How's it possible for you to have forgotten a name that's so important?" Crista wants to know.

"And you've already looked all over the barrio?" Latina asks.

She had been walking around for three hours, searching.

"It must be Providence that wanted you to be with us."

No one, either in Latina's house or in the barrio, was going to be able to locate a person without having a name to go by. The way Latina saw it, Lluvia had fallen like a blessing from heaven, like rain. And when the little girl had seen the open door, she walked right in without even knocking! There was no explanation for Chocolate not barking. "Dogs don't bark at nice people, especially a sweet little girl. You should have been named *miel* because you're just like honey or *dulce de panela*." Lluvia smiles for the first time. *God has sent her to us*, Latina thinks. Chocolate is barking at the butterflies in Lluvia's hair, not at her.

Crista thought it was possible to forget painful memories, unless someone comes along to revive them. After so many years of forgetting, Lluvia rekindled the memory of Magdalena, a memory they had been able to suppress with doses of Doctor Febles' herbal recipe.

"He CAN'T talk," Latina tells the little girl. "And if he does say something to you, you won't understand him anyway." She's talking about her grandson Bautista. The afternoon is simmering and the sky is yellow with smoke rising from the flames inside the volcano; it sets the coyote-dogs crazy, causing them to stampede toward the valley of Milagro. But there's no need for concern. "It's just Mother Nature acting up from time to time; we've fallen on some rough times of late: the volcano spitting out flames, wild animals on the loose, tremors," Latina tells her. Lluvia: "I'm so thirsty." Men disguised as animals, animals disguised as men.

With the heat and a burning sun, in Milagro de la Paz there's no such thing as being just a little thirsty. "It's probably because we live so close to that inferno." In the depths of implacable summers.

The Chaparrastique—just like an inferno. Although, it is such a pretty sight. Always belching out sulfur and smoke from the fire down inside the earth.

"When we came to Milagro from Usulután, Magdalena looked just like you. Although she was smaller. She was shy like you." *Lluvia attracts butterflies the way Magdalena attracted flowers.* "Maybe you can stay here and live with us," Latina tells her. The sky, gray with smoke as the summer drifts along on wings of goshawks on the horizon. "In my heart I hope we don't find your godmother."

Bautista wants to join them, but he knows that Lluvia won't understand his babbling, so he has no choice but to stare at her. Latina had told the little girl that they would discuss the matter when Crista got home. "She looks like me," the mother tells her.

Latina, feeling more sure of herself: "What are those butterflies doing, fluttering around like that in your hair? Don't you know they can make you go blind?"

The child tells her she's worn them in her hair ever since she was a few months old. Memories of her father and mother.

"Well, if that's true, then that's your affair." Because if a person touches a butterfly and then rubs his eyes with his fingers, "you can lose your sight."

THE YOUNGER daughter had suddenly appeared at the front door. Her step is as quick and light as a heron's. She's young, some twenty-two years of age. Angular, agile, active, and strong, the result of so much exercise, walking all day through the streets of Milagro de la Paz in order to sell their merchandise.

"She's always rushing around," the mother tells Lluvia.

Crista no sooner sees the girl than she says, "And that little thing, where'd she come from?"

Chocolate moves forward, carrying Crista's basket in his mouth. And Juan Bautista, babbling, "Crista, what did you bring me?" She's brought fruits and some scraps of food with her, but what the boy yearned for most was a good piece of meat. But he's learned to be patient, never to ask her for anything; he waits quietly until Crista offers him something. *Just seeing Crista makes my mouth water*, he tells himself in anticipation of whatever food she brought home in her basket.

"I'll explain everything to you right now," Latina says in response to Crista's question.

Crista ordered Juan Bautista to leave the room. "Go outside and play, and take the dog with you." He knows he always has to leave the room when there's something important to be discussed. "Because you're invisible," she tells him. Because he doesn't exist.

Prior to discussing the matter with her mother, Crista

begins interrogating the little girl who has remained perfectly still on the stool. The first thing that grabs the daughter's attention, her eyes being better than Latina's and the dog's, is the *chongo* Lluvia uses to tie her braids together. But she says nothing about it.

"She's the living image of your older sister," Latina affirms, stressing her words. The mother looks at Crista, hoping she'll feel moved and accept the idea of having Lluvia stay with them, at least that one day. "She has no place to sleep tonight."

"Tell me something; suppose you stay here; what kind of work can you do?" Crista asks the girl. "You're so little." While questioning the child, she softens. A certain trembling creeps into her voice when she states: "Of course, my mother says she needs you." She hasn't taken her eyes from the wings desperately fluttering in Lluvia's hair; it was as if they wanted to take flight. "It all depends on whether or not we can find your godmother."

"I know how to pick coffee beans," Lluvia says in response to Crista's question, making an effort to break out of the prison of silence that has engulfed her. She smoothes out her braids again, delicately so as not to disturb the butterflies in her *chongo*.

What good would that do them—having someone who was barely nine years old who knew how to pick coffee beans and in a house that had never seen a coffee tree? Coffee from *aguacate* seed, coffee from coffee beans, coffee from *dried* coffee leaves. Chickenshit coffee. The real coffee is only grown up there on the sides of the volcano. "We don't plant coffee and what's more we've never tasted *real* coffee," Crista tells her. But they did drink coffee twice a day. Tainted coffee. Latina and Crista agree that Lluvia can stay with them that night "until we can look for your godmother."

"I understand. Thank you very much." And it was as if a knot had been broken and all the coldness had melted away.

"Those little sparkles jumping around in your hair—what are they, anyway?" Crista finally asks her.

"They're butterflies. I've always had them," she tells Crista.

And how does she keep them from flying away? Lluvia explains to her that they've formed a nest in her hair; they're not tied down, but live there of their own free will and that she changes them every week, or rather they just fly away before dying and then others come along. Crista smiles wistfully; she doesn't know why. There's something she can't explain. Like her mother, she's unable to escape the memory of her older sister even though they feel obligated to forget her.

"And what do they eat?" Crista asks the girl, meaning the butterflies.

"*Miel silvestre.* When they're hungry, they look for flowers." And then they don't return, because they're like the flowers—beautiful, but fragile, fleeting and mortal. Whenever they go in search of their nectar, they also find death.

Crista's thoughts are in turmoil; she'd like to wipe away all trace of Magdalena's memory and she wishes Lluvia hadn't come along to upset everything, to remind her of her sister; if only she were some ordinary little girl from the volcano and nothing more.

LLUVIA HAD expressed her feelings to Latina, and she in turn told Crista: she wanted to stay. "First, let's look for your godmother," she told her. Or maybe she could stay longer since she had no place to go. She had nothing, only that little bamboo basket for a suitcase where she stored her clothes and her red coral necklace.

Latina: "We can't go out looking for her just yet."

Crista: "If you're feeling sad because you miss your

parents, then the right thing for you to do is to go back home. That way no one will be risking anything. Mama, did you explain to her yet the problems we have with the *gobernador*?"

How was she going to make that trip back to the volcano if her parents had been the ones *who wanted me to leave home*? Lluvia couldn't even imagine returning. Besides, she didn't even know what had become of her parents.

Crista: "What happened to your mama and papa?"

A long silence, waiting for the child's reply. Memory of years gone by.

"They told me they couldn't afford to keep me anymore, that I couldn't be their little girl any longer, that I should go down to Milagro de la Paz to learn how to look out for myself in the world." And the two women: "That can't be." Lluvia tells them that everyone looks out for himself as best he can, that the same thing had happened to her older sisters. For women, there's little work to be found in the fields and there's almost nothing for the men. But, in Milagro, at least a man can find work as soldier, and so the men go off to the city.

Crista, surprised: "How was it they let you come down here all by yourself?" And she kept thinking: *to this world of ours where we barely have room enough for the four of us: two women, a boy, and a dog.* "And us, with nothing to offer you!" she adds.

These are good people, the little girl thinks.

Latina, puffing away on her Copán cigar—the Honduran tobacco she likes so much—hasn't missed a word between her daughter and Lluvia. She interjects: "Let her be for now. Stop asking so many questions. She'll tell us more tomorrow."

Crista does as her mother says, even though she's not sure if there'll even be a tomorrow or if they'll ever find the girl's godmother.

"How old are you?" Crista asks, intervening again.

"I'll be nine soon."

"When?" Latina asks, walking over to Crista.

"I don't know, but I'll be nine."

My God, Latina mutters, talking to herself as she waves the smoke from the *puro* away from her long dress.

"And at your age, you're on your own in this world?" The little girl, with total poise, and touching the butterflies from time to time, says she's used to it. "Up there on the Chaparrastique, I had to walk a long way to get to the coffee fields."

Or to hunt animals. "My mama and papa didn't always go with me." Crista, insisting on knowing more, asks: "How old were you when you started working in the coffee fields?"

"Ever since I was little," Lluvia replies, as sure of herself as someone who had lived a thousand years.

In the distance, Milagro's tower clock strikes six. The hour for evening prayers. Latina, responding immediately to the call, begins moving her lips in a silent litany. The incandescent sun, looking like a flaming red flower, disappears into the mouth of the Chaparrastique.

Crista reiterates that the best thing for the girl to do is return home; she could follow someone, an ox-cart driver, one of those who goes up to the volcano to bring back coffee. Lluvia says she won't go back home because then she'd be going against her destiny.

Crista is surprised: "How does someone as young as you know about something like destiny?"

And the child answers that she has known about such things ever since she was little because it was something her parents talked about all the time.

Latina knows that tomorrow is another day and she can ask Lluvia all the questions she wants then; she feels certain she'll stay with them, at least for the night, to have a place to sleep. "If the soldiers come, I'll just tell them she's my daughter."

WHEN CRISTA makes her rounds of Milagro's streets, selling roses and the apparel they sew at home, she's following in Magdalena's footsteps. As early as seven in the morning, she needs to be at the corner where the hospital is located, to be ready for the young girls on their way to the city's two parochial schools because they often take a flower for their teacher. The roses are pretty. Once Crista has sold all the flowers, she sets off for the market, her basket filled with the clothes they sell to the campesinos. She doesn't come home until three or four in the afternoon and then she sits down to make more clothes for the next day. Her work can take her late into the night, especially if business was good that day; if she succeeded in selling enough merchandise, then she could buy the additional fabrics she needed for expanding their business. The rainy season and the first months of the summer are better for them because there's more work for the farmers and they have money to buy the clothes she and her mother make.

By the time the whistle at the yarn factory has blown, Crista has come home with her basket filled with fruits or something special for dinner, like spare ribs. *It makes my mouth water,* Juan Bautista tells himself. Spare ribs roasted over wood coals, seasoned with *tomate* and some hot chile.

At night, Crista barely says a word—next to nothing, even though she feels the need to talk to someone. She always concentrates on what needs to be done and so she doesn't say a word to Juan Bautista who is thrilled to have some spare ribs for dinner. *I'll eat all the meat off the bones until they're just as white as can be.* Crista can't think about anything else except her work and openly displays her cares in front of the family—from the time she gets up early in the morning until she goes to bed at night when she hears the tower clock strike nine. Moreover, she markets her merchandise seven days a week, no matter what: on festival days, on holidays, even on birthdays and holy days. God forgives her because survival comes first.

Her mother always told her: "In this life, we only have two occasions we commemorate: birth and death." Both were milestones and were always observed, one with joy and the other with solemnity. That was how it was and there was no reason for a person to think otherwise. That was the only life they knew, so there was no reason for making comparisons. The thread of life just keeps on unwinding. A person is born, grows up, works, and takes care of himself until he comes to the end. It's only on this final occasion that people look to God for an answer, an explanation. "He brings us into the world and He decides when it's our time to leave it," Latina liked to say. Crista feels no resentment because she's never even considered the possibility of comparing her limited prospects with something else. She knows she loves those who she has at her side, but she doesn't ask herself what love is. She just loves, without knowing what it really means. To love: it's like breathing and drinking water, but the word "love" was never spoken in their house.

In Milagro de la Paz survival meant having enough water to drink. Water and breathing, it was all one and the same. Even believing in God didn't surpass those two things in importance. It had never even occurred to them to mention the word *love*; it didn't exist in their vocabulary. For them, death, hate, and evil were the ever recurring topics.

"Mama, why doesn't anyone in our house have a birthday?" Crista asks.

"We have birthdays. The thing of it is that we just don't give them any thought."

THERE'S NO doubt in her mind that Lluvia is Magdalena. She likes to talk and that pleases Latina. The grandson: *I don't talk to Crista because she doesn't understand me.*

Lluvia's parents had explained to her that if they weren't ever able to support her and thought she had no decent future there with them, then it would be better for her to leave and go find another way to start a new life, like going down to Milagro. At least, in Milagro a young girl could find a job, put some food on the table, and earn her keep if she worked hard. And she could share her heartaches and her experiences with others, maybe even help others with the goodness she had to give. What Lluvia doesn't understand yet is that she's going to be living the same life Magdalena had, the older daughter whom Latina needed to erase from her memory.

The grandson had even taken Magdalena's picture with him out back to the privy, claiming that's where she comes to visit him, a secret only Lluvia knew about, and then Latina and Crista suspected as much and now they had proof. Juan Bautista firmly believes Magdalena visits him there, but Latina, familiar with her grandson's imagination, takes it in stride.

"You've got to forget Magdalena; she's dead. The only place she exists now is in Juan Bautista's head," Latina tells her daughter.

Crista heeds her mother on this matter, but it's the only instance where she's submissive. And she tries not to remember the past. Still, she has moments when she sees things more clearly and can conceive of trading places with her older sister.

Lluvia explains to the women that she wasn't really such

a stranger to Milagro de la Paz; she was always gazing down at the city, in the Siramá River Valley, at the red-tiled roofs of the houses, a coral red like the necklace she kept stored in her little basket; at night, she liked looking at the sky above and the sky below, one filled with aqua green lights and wandering stars—*a mansion for the soul*—and the other filled with bright yellow lights, which was Milagro de la Paz. "You can't get lost," her parents had told her. After all, there was only one road leading down there and, at the end of it, she'd see the cemetery. "They weren't home when I left, but my older sisters sent me off with their blessing."

Latina returns to the kitchen area and leaves Crista alone with the little girl. "Come over here. Help me water the flowers."

"MILAGRO HAS a few things to offer, but it also takes. Don't think it's so easy living here," Crista tells the girl. Recently they had been threatened by the coyote-dogs, just to give her one example. "I don't want to scare you, but we have to let you know how things are."

And that's how Crista talks to her at some length while Latina prepares the meal and Juan Bautista plays in the patio with the dog.

"And exactly where do your mama and papa live on the Chaparrastique?"

"We lived in a house near the crater."

Latina associates the mouth of the volcano with hell's gate and she grimaces.

"What's the matter?" her daughter asks. "You're trembling."

"I was thinking about death," the mother replies.

Crista says that if a little girl can live up there on the volcano, then there's no reason to be afraid of the crater or hell's gate. "We've got enough troubles as it is without giving ourselves one more thing to worry about." Then, turning to the girl: "Explain to me how you could forget your godmother's name." Lluvia says her parents had told her the name and she was sure her godmother lived here. Coming down that mountain for what seemed like an eternity, she had reached Milagro de la Paz. Crista resigns herself to the situation: "That's all right; as far as I'm concerned, I don't see a problem." It was lucky for her she had come to their house. "It's a good thing for you we're decent people and there's no one here but us." Bautista is playing with Chocolate.

"And what do your mama and papa do?" Practically the same answers: they used to cut coffee in the coffee fields and plant corn. She always speaks in the past tense because she's sure she'll never see them again. For a little girl, the road leading down from the volcano is a path with no return.

Crista shivers. "All of a sudden I feel a cold breeze coming off the volcano." And with it comes the howling of the coyote-dogs; they sound close by. "We ought to go inside. Don't be afraid, though; when the howls sound so close, they're really not."

But the fear was there all the same; it seemed as if the *coyotes* were stalking the house. Then, with a change in direction of the wind, the howling stopped.

Lluvia, in answer to Crista's question about her parents: "I don't know what they do now. I don't know if they're even alive."

Now it's the fluttering of the butterflies that dominates the silence.

THE THREE women are sitting outside, chatting, while Juan Bautista and the dog are playing next to the privy.

Crista: "Well, the Lord wanted you to find my mama."

Lluvia, after a moment's thought: "I feel like I've found my home." Crista plays the devil's advocate: "It seems to me you made all that up about a godmother." She realizes she has accused the little girl of lying. In a hushed voice she asks for forgiveness.

Then she changes the subject again: "Is it true you came in without knocking first?" She makes a point of explaining that Chocolate didn't attack her because he's not full-grown yet. The little girl tells Crista she's not afraid of dogs.

Crista: "You know what? It's still cold here." And she calls to Latina to put some coffee on. Lluvia didn't feel the cold and so she didn't want any coffee. Latina: "Children don't drink coffee at night because then they wet the bed."

They all ponder their own thoughts. Lluvia: *Even Latina thinks my mama and papa made that up about my godmother.* "And as for my name, I know that in this world no one is called Lluvia," she tells Crista, who interrupts her: "What can you possibly know about the world?" But Lluvia continues explaining: "A person has to be called by the name she's christened with." Crista says she thought the church didn't bother with the people on the volcano.

"The missionaries go up there every five years," Latina says as she gets up and goes over to poke around in Crista's basket that's sitting out on a little pinewood table. Crista reproaches her mother for only talking about things that arouse fear. "All Crista and I know about the world is what Chele Pintura used to tell us," Latina tells her.

They stop talking momentarily. Crista is watching Lluvia, examining her more with her instincts than with her eyes. She, too, seemed to recognize something familiar in her; perhaps she saw in her the cherished image of her older sister. Crista: "How is that butterflies have taken such a fancy to you?" Lluvia's sunflower-patterned *chongo* is fluttering in the air. "I never had any toys to play with, so I made friends with the butterflies," she explains. Crista suddenly realizes that an hour has gone by since she came home and that, in talking with Lluvia, the time has slipped away from her, and now her bladder is burning. "Keep on watering while I go pee." She leaves Lluvia by herself, tending to the roses. Latina is off to the side, cooking some spare ribs. Crista runs to the privy, a tiny shed at the far end of the patio.

On returning, she tells the girl: "Let's eat, because it's getting late for me." She's thinking about all the work she has to do that evening.

When the time was right, her mother had taught her how to sew. She sews everyday, beginning at dusk. As they leave the rose garden, Crista tells Lluvia, "Don't worry about anything; you'll stay with us tonight. We're not going to abandon you." The plan was for Crista to go out the next day with her mother to ask around and see if anybody might know anything about a *cipota* named Lluvia. "We have to be careful about this or we'll give her away," Crista says. The grandmother, from the back, standing at the *fogón*: "You see how things are in this house. We have to help each other." *God punishes a person many times for his mistakes.* Latina: "We'll all be running a risk if the soldiers find out you're living here."

The little girl said her godmother means nothing to her. "But, you do," she tells the two women.

Latina calls out to them to come and eat. They approach the pinewood table. Latina, who really doesn't want Lluvia to leave, tells her daughter that tomorrow's another day, that now it's time to eat in peace and give God thanks; at least, they have a few scraps of meat on the table. There're even some beans. *If Crista refuses to accept Lluvia, it's as if she wants to rid herself of Magdalena,* Latina thinks when she hears the younger daughter voice her fears and her doubts about this. On the other hand, perhaps it was a good sign that Crista was acting that way, not insisting on Lluvia staying with them; the mother reasons that it must be because she had not really made any association between the little girl and her older sister.

Several years ago they had made an agreement: they wouldn't bring up anything related either to Magdalena's tragedy or to the hardships they had experienced since her death. "One day the world will be within our reach." They associated the world with abundance and dreams, the way Chele Pintura had described it in telling them about his adventures.

Their first meal together. "May it not be our last," Latina says. Crista serves Bautista first; his eyes are as big as saucers as he looks at the spare ribs she has placed in front of him. And Chocolate is at his side, salivating.

THE TWO WOMEN are conversing in the dark mist that hangs over the room. "Someone asked about Lluvia," Latina says. She doesn't want to say who. Crista: "It must have been one of her relatives from the volcano." "She doesn't have any relatives," the mother replies. All her family relations had disappeared. "A person never knows what can happen." Crista: "Don't talk like that. There's no need to fear what we don't know."

The two women try to sleep, but they continue to talk. A murmuring of words, expressions of emotion, like poems from other worlds. Sounds of crickets and termites. Crista insists that Latina tell her who came to look for the little girl.

"Doña Matilde says some soldiers from Casamata came by her store, asking if there was another person living here. There's no reason to worry; they never knew how many we were to begin with."

"This sort of thing frightens me; I can't live with it," says Crista. The soldiers keep vigil in the barrio by order of the military governor and one of the rules is that only family members can occupy a single dwelling; residence is prohibited to people from outside or those without papers. The army has been given the duty of maintaining order; that's their job.

Well, the only outsider here in las Angustias is Lluvia. If the soldiers are asking about anyone, it's got to be her. Latina is always thinking the worst, but she keeps it to herself; that way, she can feel better about things when the worst doesn't come to pass. And if the worst does happen, then she has already prepared herself for it.

Matilde had told the soldiers she didn't know of any outsider who might be working there, that the only people living in las Angustias were family members, that they should go search the barrios in the center of the city. "Why are they afraid to go poking around in the other barrios? Why only in las Angustias?" Matilde asks Latina. "Maybe because there've been more problems in las Angustias," Latina asserts. "Dead bodies in the streets, the *coyotes.* It's so isolated here, and the soldiers, that's what keeps order in las Angustias," she adds. "Yes, but they bring the corpses here from other places to get rid of them," Matilde says. The area has a bad reputation. Latina: "It's not our fault."

Matilde: "I made them understand there aren't any outsiders working in las Angustias because the families that live here barely have enough food for themselves as it is, much less anything to spare for a stranger." The soldiers regard her kindly, the way they would their own mothers; Matilde's words don't trouble them. When all is said and done, they know they're on good terms with her and that she's not a person who ever causes problems for anybody.

"And who told you we're looking for someone?" And she answers evasively, saying she was only surmising, and tells them she'll bring them some coffee before it gets cold. The soldiers treat her with respect; after all, they don't have any reason to doubt the owner of the little store. They lean their backs against the wall, near the door, and sip their coffee.

Latina asked her if they said anything about extending their search to other houses. "They didn't say anything, Latina, because they never know anything themselves; what I do remember is that they said they were looking for the *unknowns* who've been going around killing people and that they're here to protect us. And that no one should be worried, that they do this from time to time because almost everybody from the barrio goes to her store, that this was only routine work for them."

Crista, with conviction: "The best thing is for the girl not to leave the house, not to go out to buy anything, not even to the store; just you, mama, you'll be the one who does all the shopping, like always" she tells Latina. "Who are the *unknowns*, anyway?" Latina wonders. Matilde: "No one knows; maybe it's the coyote-dogs themselves." Latina: "This much I know: they're murderers."

And so the house and the patio became Lluvia's entire world.

THEY HAD been living under a state of emergency for years. What started it was the reputation the residents of las Angustias had acquired, especially the women who stood in front of the military governor's house and protested against the expropriation of their *ejidos*—a semicircle of common property surrounding Milagro that looked like a half-moon. But, that had happened many years ago. "I wasn't even born then," Matilde says. "Me neither. Besides, we're from Usulután," Latina remarks. They burned down the comandante's house and then they lynched him; they cut off his penis and stuffed it in his mouth. It was the women who led the assault and ever since then, they were feared and hated. That was more than fifty years ago.

"They don't forget," Matilde tells her. "Where you're living now, most of this land was common property," she continues. "They threw the people off and moved them to the foot of the Chaparrastique where there were only rocks and lava. Some built their houses on top of those rocks and dug through to the soil in order to plant trees. In time, everything settled down, and what was left behind were groups of unidentified assassins who go around at night, stealing and murdering."

Despite the proximity of the troops at Casamata, the

unknowns, making themselves out to be animals with the sounds they made, were more clever than the soldiers and were able to taunt them; the troops never managed to catch anybody. At the same time, others believed those animals were the soldiers themselves in disguise, going around avenging that execution of the *gobernador* fifty years ago. In other words, they were the kind who don't forget. "We pay a high price for the sins of others," Latina says. "The truth: we get blamed for everything as long as we're alive."

Rather than send patrols on long journeys, it was decided that a permanent military post be established in las Angustias, a kind of headquarters which they named La Casamata. The soldiers became a familiar sight in the barrio once they began patrolling the streets; they'd start out at four in the morning, chanting and shouting orders. On their way back to the barracks, they stop at Matilde's little store where they buy *pan dulce* and get treated to some hot coffee; in effect, they were the defenders of order, and Matilde couldn't complain about how they treated her; they were respectful and paid for what they wanted rather than pilfer anything from her shelves. Or else they spread out, going from house to house in small patrols, but those visits became nothing more than courtesy calls of a sort in which they could get small gifts from the neighbors, everything from fruits to eggs. The residents feel flattered when the soldiers address them in a nice way and show good manners, especially since it's coming from men who, by the very nature of their work, have always inspired fear and respect.

THOSE WHO BUILT their houses on top of the lava formations were told they could stay; as for those who wanted to remain on the land, they would have to buy back the property from the State or from one of the nine landowners. That's what the law said. A person had to be in possession of the property and hold a property title issued by the governor. "Imagine, having to buy back what used to belong to everybody, the common land." The same thing had happened in Usulután. Those who were the strongest became landowners overnight; the comandante carried out the law. Power comes from the barrel of a rifle. Everybody had fenced in his parcel of land with stones from the volcano, but that still wasn't proof of anything; a person had to show the signed paper, the official documentation of ownership. But, how were they going to have papers if the order came down overnight and no one knew where to go to request them. "That was when the women of Milagro de la Paz rose up." No one was expecting a violent reaction. "And what did the men do?" asks Latina. "I don't know. They stayed home, looking after the children," Matilde explains. "They thought because they were women nothing was going to happen to them."

Those who could, put up houses, either of adobe or reeds and mud, and with palm frond roofs. "That's how las Angustias was born," Matilde explains. Those who didn't manage to put up fences were told to get out. That had been the governor's idea, to sneak up on them and catch them by surprise; anyone who didn't comply with the terms for legalizing his holdings saw everything confiscated. "People thought their stone fences would be all they needed." Ever since then, the fences built out of the black lava from the Chaparrastique have been a characteristic of the properties that border Milagro. Even after it was admitted that they were the rightful owners, they suffered intimidation all the same; and those who rebelled simply disappeared and were never heard from again. The ones who were lucky and had the fortitude to put up with the threats, managed to stay on. As a result, much of the remaining population of Angustias consisted of those who had successfully resisted. The strongest had survived at the cost of now being the weakest. Reality had immunized them against the consequences of the laws of the republic.

A certain saying was born of their experience: "Half-alive and half-dead." It was like living on the edge of an abyss where humility and patience were in some way the only hope a person had. Nothing affected them more than a certain propensity they had for fearing the night, even though they had come to accept that as a part of their everyday life.

That all had happened fifty years ago. And now the people of Milagro de la Paz have been accepted, although they're still stigmatized by their proximity to that dark past of disobedience to the law regarding property rights. Each day passes and fades into oblivion. What good does it do to remember? "The fact is, it was a law of confiscation," Matilde explains.

"We've got to live every minute of every day that God gives us life." Not uncommon words in the mouths of those who lived in the tree-lined patios and the simple one-room-houses of las Angustias, that great world of people. It was better to forget Milagro's crushing history.

The only pockets of resonance in the nocturnal hours are the crickets and the termites. At other times, it's the flight of an owl. Or the faintly perceptible rumblings from the volcano that, during cycles, unleashes veritable bombardments above Milagro. Or the howling of the coyote-dogs.

THEY'RE ALL AWAKE in the house. The grandmother has set out a *huacal* of water by the door to prevent the evil spirits from getting in; waiting for the tower clock to chime nine times, no one wants to go to sleep. She doesn't speak to them about *the unknowns*, but about the soldiers from the

Casamata barracks who could show up unexpectedly after dark. And because those who came calling at night were considered evil spirits, the way to keep them out was to place a bowl of salted water by the door and, on the other side, a picture of El Salvadorcito del Mundo, the curly-haired Savior of the World, in a carved wood frame. "Protect us, Salvadorcito del Mundo, you who are so good to the poor," Latina prays.

That's how the fear of the darkness is born.

"For heaven's sake, no one's going to eat them," Crista tells her mother as she lights the way for the children to get into bed. "Let them be; you're the one who makes them afraid." Especially at four in the morning, when the voices of the soldiers can be heard, chanting military slogans to fortify their courage and their spirit. Trotting about the barrio, *looking out for us so there won't be any trouble here.*

CRISTA HELPS the grandmother light the fire, and that's the only time she hums her melodies; also when she washes the utensils. Sometimes the grandmother complains about her singing such gloomy songs.

"I don't know any happy ones, and as for you, all you ever sing is La Caza del Cusuco, which makes us laugh because of the way you dance to it," Crista says. *The Armadillo Hunt.*

Once she has finished her chores, she goes over to the *fogón* while Latina trims the threads from the clothes they've worked on. When it comes time to stop their work, they wake Bautista, who is fast asleep on a *petate*; he's hardly an infant anymore. Both women are dead with fatigue. Or half-dead. Before going to bed, Crista looks around to make sure the *fogón* has been properly cleaned. "We can't leave any ashes," she reminds her mother. Ashes are an enticement to the evil spirits that come and play tricks on people. The grandmother can't rest easy until they've completed that task and so she works alongside Crista to get it done. In fact, it was Latina who got her daughter into the habit. Crista puts her scissors away. "The most valuable thing I own in this life," she mutters. Each one retires to her own dark corner of the room. Both women carefully check the beds. Spiders fall from the ceiling when a storm wind blows. Afterwards the grandmother will prepare their daily dose of herbal tea. To numb their memories.

THEY HAD known some very rough times, times when they had nothing.

"We've got to save every last *centavo* so we never have to go around begging anybody for anything," the mother tells her older daughter. Those were days when they had even less; besides, who could lend anybody anything if all the people were in the same straits? "If we can't sell the clothes, maybe we can find a way to sell fruits or vegetables, and if we can't do that, we can sell stones," the grandmother says sarcastically.

"We can't make much selling fruits," Magdalena says and she adds: "We could get some pigs and fatten them up, but where would we get them anyway if we don't have any money to buy them?" Then, in an effort to bolster her own spirits: "Maybe when the summer comes, things will get better," she says, trying to sound hopeful.

"If the campesinos don't have work, we'll go hungry and starve," the grandmother laments. During the rainy months, the campesinos can sow corn in their little *milpa* fields, to feed their families if nothing else, but they can't earn any money on the farms. Then they don't come into Milagro to buy what they need.

Recently they weren't having much success selling their

clothes. "The little we earn isn't enough to feed four mouths." The three of them and the dog. "Too bad we don't have one less mouth to feed," Magdalena says. The mother quickly responds: "Ave María Purísima, Holy Mother of God, don't even think such a thing." The daughter knows she has said the wrong thing, but insists they have to find another way to make some money.

They're nestled underneath their blankets, under a tile roof, inside four adobe walls, enough to protect them from changes in the weather; a strong house, capable of resisting the heavy August rains or the November winds, whirlwinds that sometimes can lift the tiles off the roof just like sheets of paper.

Added to all their troubles were the rumblings from the volcano. Latina: "When the Chaparrastique starts popping off like that, there's no place to hide." They lived under the threat of the Chaparrastique, but Milagro de la Paz wasn't going to disappear; it had survived for more than five hundred years.

Magdalena protests: "You don't have to talk that way; you always scare me at night. You talk different during the day, mama." The mother continues pondering things while puffing on her cigar. Magdalena and Latina share the same bed. The older daughter: "Really, we ought be brave enough to go outside and sleep in the patio; I'd rather be eaten by the coyote-dogs than get crushed inside these walls."

The world of the patio, the universe of the well, and the fruit trees. Everything is so immense and so small at the same time.

Providence smiled on them after Magda found some live rose stems and decided to try her fortune. She would plant the cuttings to see if they would take root and, if they did, have a garden.

FROM THE TIME we got up this morning, Lluvia hasn't taken her eyes off me; she's over there looking like a statue in Barrios Park, and when I look at her, she pretends she's not watching me. Lluvia is in the *asoleadero*, spreading out her clothes on the rocks under the hot sun. Bautista is watering the roses. *When I'm finished, I'll pick some fruit from the marañón tree. I climb the cashew tree and I see she's still watching, but she doesn't look up for fear I'll fall.* It's better that way because Lluvia can't see him, but he sees her. *She's down there, washing clothes and doesn't know I'm up here in the marañón; she always looks for me in the naranjo.* He looks out toward the laundry area and then glances toward the mound of garbage—a miniature volcano, trying to see if Magdalena's there; she hasn't been to see him for two days. "I'm not going to visit you for a few days; Lluvia or my mother or Crista could discover us." After he eats his third cashew, he hears Lluvia's voice calling him: "Muchacho, you're going to get hurt." *I argue with her:* how does she know what I'm doing? She shouldn't be watching him, anyway. The little girl doesn't answer; she is annoyed with him and concentrates on spreading out her clothes to dry on the rocks.

Then I take a closer look and I see that she's shaking. I ask her if she'd like some fruit. She looks up at the orange tree, but then she remembers a person shouldn't do that, because of the danger: if you see someone in a tree, the person could fall. She wipes her face with her apron. Lluvia's mood is different today. Bautista climbs down from the tree and goes over to her. He offers her a cashew, but Lluvia doesn't want it; she doesn't like the way they taste. She turns and walks away, and he follows her; they start going around each other in circles; she, offering him her back and he trying to see her face; using their bodies as the axis, it looks like a dance of spinning tops, the *trompos* children like to play with. "What's the matter?" he asks. "It scares me to see you cry." Lluvia finally answers: "I heard the *coyotes* howling in the distance." She isn't telling him the truth; the fact is the night before she had heard Latina say that Magda wasn't Bautista's mother.

When Latina returned from Doña Matilde's store, they tell her about the animals howling in the distance and the grandmother confirms what Bautista had just said: it can't be the coyote-dogs because they only come out at night. Lluvia grows calmer. *Although, it could be los seres desconocidos*, Latina tells herself even though she knows they haven't come around for the past six years.

JUAN BAUTISTA was always alluding to his fears; whether they were genuine or not, he needed to express them either in words or actions. *I like to cry because my tears keep me company.* But, he didn't like it when others cried because then he felt confused. Lluvia grabs hold of him by his curly hair and caresses him, but turns her head so he can't see her face. He squeezes her hand and asks: "What's wrong?" And she keeps her face turned away from him. She's angry and tells him to leave her alone. "Let me be" in a tone of voice that frightened him more than her crying, but he doesn't let on that he's scared and he tries to console her. Then Juan Bautista returns to the cashew tree with every intention of staying there or moving on to the orange tree where people and feelings can't reach him. To forget about Lluvia and to transform himself into the solitary guardian of the oranges. And this time his heart tells him he has made himself invisible to her. *Just the way I make myself invisible to Crista.*

THAT WAS the same day the soldiers showed up. They had come down from the volcano. "We double-timed it for three hours from the top," they said. From the crest of the Chaparrastique all the way down to the cemetery and then into the Angustias barrio itself. And they were thirsty. *We're all sick to our stomachs with fear; the soldiers can take Lluvia away just because she wasn't born in this house.* They came, asking for water. Later, the grandmother told Bautista that no one except them knew the truth about Lluvia, whether or not she belonged to them; well, there was also Doña Matilde, but she wasn't going to say anything. And the soldiers left just the way they had arrived—double-timing it. Bautista: "Why do the soldiers run at night?" Latina had answered him: "They want to be strong." Bautista: "Will they come looking for Lluvia?" Latina: "Maybe." The boy: "Why?" Because she hadn't been born in that house; only family members are permitted to live in las Angustias. The day the soldiers showed up: *Maybe they've only come to ask for some water.* They saw Lluvia, but she looked like she belonged to the family. "What a pretty little thing the old lady's got here. You didn't tell us." Latina thinks the soldiers have been good of late, but sometimes they still behaved like what they were, like soldiers. She doesn't react to what they say. "Thanks, *abuela.*" Politely: "You're welcome." Then to herself: *Here's your granny, right here between my legs, under my slip.*

BY THE LIGHT of the yellow candles, their flames flickering: "You know what I eat at this time of night," the grandmother says resolutely, in answer to her daughter's chiding: "Oh, for goodness sake, mama! Already eating your tobacco. You act as if you're still hungry." Crista knows her mother only chews tobacco when she is in bed, but this time she's doing it while scurrying back and forth in the house, arranging imaginary things, moving the utensils from one side to the other, changing their positions.

Latina: "You know I don't chew tobacco because I'm hungry."

"You're sad, then," Crista replies.

"I'm just thinking."

"You don't have to punish yourself for what's happened; there's no way for the soldiers to find out that Lluvia came down from the volcano."

"I didn't say I'm punishing myself, just thinking," Latina affirms. "Tell me something. What would happen if they found out? Do you think they'd take her away?"

"Oh, mama! Let's not worry about something we can't control. They're not going to do anything to us for taking Lluvia in." Besides, they weren't going to go around telling anybody about it.

"You know it's against the law to take in strangers," Latina reiterates. Her fifty-three years of experience as a survivor give her reason for concern.

"It's against the law, but we know there's nothing wrong about Lluvia living with us. God's laws are different," Crista asserts in a defensive tone.

Latina: "The soldiers say the trouble with us is that we don't respect their laws."

"Laws they've made. We don't have to respect those laws."

"Maybe if they were good laws, we'd accept them," Latina says, not totally convinced.

"As long as we're living under their rules, we've got to go along with what they say," Crista says, resigned.

"All right. If it comes to it, we'll fight for our rights. This is our house and we don't have to ask for anybody's permission for somebody else to live here, especially somebody we like," says Latina, gathering more courage the more she talks.

"They always find some excuse; they'll say we've taken in a whole family, not just one person," Crista reasons. Despite her best efforts, she can't hide her fear.

Latina: "In any case, we've got to hide Lluvia. If we don't, someone could be watching us and make trouble; it's like fighting shadows."

"You're right, mama. We've survived until now because we've known how to look out for ourselves."

"Or maybe we've just been lucky."

"Being patient has paid off for us, too."

"And God is good," the mother adds.

Crista, with bitterness in her voice: "Sometimes He forgets we even exist."

Latina: "Don't say such a thing; God punishes a person for talking that way."

"God doesn't punish someone who's done nothing wrong."

"That's true, but all the same, you don't have to say what you said out loud," Latina says, crossing herself, with a deep uneasiness etched on her face.

LLUVIA IS doing the laundry while Bautista hauls up the water. She is slapping the clothes against a rock to rinse out the water before she lays them out to dry on the stones of the *asoleadero*.

"How many buckets are you going to haul up?" Lluvia asks.

"The same as always: fifteen. Why? Are you going to help me?"

"I can't, but I'd like you to do me a little favor and haul up two more buckets."

"My hands hurt; I've got blisters on them."

After he finished hauling up another bucket of water and emptying it into the big clay pot, he held out his hands for her to see them.

"Let me take a look," Lluvia says.

The two youngsters are standing under a tree, framed by the leaves and branches that spread out against the clear summer sky. He shows Lluvia his hands. Small blisters on the palms and on the tips of the fingers. "That hurts. Don't squeeze them." They glance over at the stone fence. Birds in flight in the perennial blue sky.

"And what do you do to keep your hands soft?" he asks her.

"I rub them with spit and *caca de gallina*." Chicken shit.

"Can you help me?"

"Maybe. It's a secret I learned when I lived on the volcano, if that's all right with you," Lluvia tells him.

"Can you rub some spit and *caca de gallina* on mine?"

Lluvia laughs for the first time since she arrived.

"Don't be stupid. You have to do it with your own spit; if I do it with mine, it can get infected."

"All right; when I'm finished hauling the last bucket, I'm going to rub some spit and *caca de gallina* on them," he tells her.

WHILE BAUTISTA is spitting on his hands, Lluvia picks up the empty bucket and with one motion drops it down into the well. "I'm just going to haul up the other two buckets of water I need to finish the laundry." Then Bautista begins pulling up the extra buckets she needs. He does it quickly, imitating Lluvia's technique. She observes him before returning to the laundry area, when all of a sudden he places his hands on the well's rim behind him and jumps into a sitting position.

Lluvia screams: “My God!”

“What’s the matter?”

“Nothing. I thought you were going to fall in. If you do that again, you’re really going to get me upset.”

“I want to look at the water.”

She tells him not to do that again, ever. With his feet dangling over the outer edge, he turns his head to look down into the humid well, filled with ferns.

“Can you see the water?” she asks him.

“Yes, I can see it,” he tells her, pleased with himself.

“Why’s it so important for you to see the water down there?”

“So I can see the stars in the daytime.”

“Why do you want to see the stars now when you can see them at night?”

“It’s not the same thing.”

“You’re such a daffy little boy,” Lluvia says, leaning over the edge of the well. “I don’t see anything.”

“You have to wait until your eyes get used to it. It’s dark down there.”

Now Lluvia is lying face down on the ledge of the well; she remains perfectly still so that it almost appears she’s fallen asleep there; then after a few minutes she lets out a scream and jumps down, saying, “It’s true, it’s true, there’re stars down there. It’s incredible.” A person could see them in the water in plain daylight.

In the west, the sun has begun its descent and moves directly toward the volcano, where it disappears, leaving a trail of flaming red streaks that the wind will push out to sea, cleansing the sky and making way for a night illuminated by the cold fire of thousands of moons and stars shrouded in mist.

JUAN BAUTISTA asks Latina about Magda: "Why did she leave us?"

"She didn't want to go away; she died." But that isn't what he wants to hear even though he's afraid to ask. The night before he had heard the two women talking. "We don't talk at night; I'm the one who talks, but I talk to myself, so I don't know why you should say you heard me."

At that moment Latina was thinking about the one thing her grandson wanted to know and she thought it important, but it was better for him not to know or else she might confuse him more. *He'd be better off if he'd stop poking his nose around at night.* The grandmother thinks he must be getting up at night to listen to them; how else could the child know the things she and Crista talked about?

"I heard you say that Magdalena isn't my mother," he says mournfully as soon as she comes to join him in the privy. "What you heard was your imagination telling you things," Latina answers. And she thought about explaining a few things to him to help him understand, "because I don't know, this child could end up going crazy with all that he imagines," she tells Crista, who covers her ears to show that she doesn't want to hear any more about Magdalena. It had been five years of forgetting and now Lluvia comes along and Magdalena is reincarnated. The memory of her sister is a torment for her.

When Bautista asks Latina how Magdalena died, she remains silent. It wasn't necessary for him to know. "Stop it, please. You scare me with your questions." But he keeps wanting to know if Nicolás was his father. She tells him again that Nicolás doesn't exist.

In that case, Juan Bautista wouldn't tell her he had found

himself face to face with Magdalena, that he had seen her in the distance, beyond the mounds of trash, leaping over the fence of lava rocks that separated them from the adjacent lot where the municipal dump was located. *My mother's alive. "I exist only for you. Agreed?" Magdalena told me.* The only condition for them staying together, even if it were only in the privy, was that he had to keep the secret. "Why is it everybody's got a gripe about something? It's as if they can't accept the way God brought them into the world," Latina comments.

He wasn't ever going to tell anyone about those visits, not after his grandmother had finally told him outright that Magdalena was dead and that she wasn't his mother. He pursues the subject with Latina, hoping she'll tell him that she lied. Both are sitting together in the *asoleadero*. Latina: *A child shouldn't call his mother a liar.* But she doesn't have the strength to scold him.

She feels free of her old torment now. It'd be better for him to know the truth and put an end to his illusions.

She's alive for me, too. But I don't have any illusions about it; on the contrary, I try to forget her. But, she was also becoming aware that the effect of the *aguas azules* was beginning to diminish. More and more her mind was stirring with memories of Magdalena.

"I DON'T know what you're going to do with all these books," the mother tells Magda, sounding very contrary.

"Some day they'll do somebody some good; that's my hope. There has to be more to life than this—just the three of us and a dog," she says, referring to her mother, her little sister Crista, herself, and Plutón.

"This is the path I've had to walk with the two of you," Latina says.

"A person makes her own path in life, mama."

Later, when Chele came to the house, the pact is sealed and Magda tells him: "That's fine. Go ahead and put the books over there." At first, he had asked them to keep the two boxes for him because he didn't have enough room for them. But Latina was opposed "because books attract all kinds of vermin," she mutters. Then Chele said he was giving them the books as a gift; they were of no use to him, anyway; he was just holding onto them. Books were meant to be read and her two daughters were in school now. Besides, Latina had offered him some work and invited him to eat with them. "I'm all alone too, just like the three of you," he tells them.

A man and three women, wrapped in the somnolence of a tree-shaded patio, between the shriek of a hawk and the clucking of hens.

"It's best we have some agreement, Chele. We can't be accepting any gifts this way," says Magdalena, who doesn't want any obligations to someone who has seen so much of the world. That would be like hiring a man from some other planet.

The most difficult part was overcoming Latina's resist ance. "There's no time for reading in this house," she says. "We're only doing this to help you out, Chele," Magdalena says and she reaffirms their invitation for him to come two days a week to have something to eat with them in exchange for the books. Latina: "Let's be clear on this much: we only eat vegetables; most of the time, *chipilín* soup with eggs." The man accepts; that way he'd be able to socialize with the women, especially with Magdalena for whom he feels a certain indefinable love, one that's timid and unsure, as if she were made of crystal and flesh at the same time.

The mother tells Crista to take the books from Chele. "You're not allowed to look at them; they're for grown-ups," she tells the child. Crista-child shows her displeasure, but does as her mother tells her; Chele isn't to her liking, although ever since she started learning things in school, she's felt a natural inclination for reading, more out of curiosity, though, because up until now she has had only one book in her hands: the primer, a combination of Catholic prayers and moral instruction, illustrated with drawings of suffering Church martyrs who were either shot through with arrows or being devoured by beasts.

"All right, Chele, the boxes are heavy, so help the child slide them under the bed."

Chele Pintura, followed by Crista-child, carries the boxes across the room and, before pushing them under the bed belonging to the mother and the older daughter, he lays one of the books aside, one that has a thick dust jacket; Crista-child notices it and asks him why he's leaving that one out and Chele explains how the grandmother told him this book wasn't part of their agreement. Crista-child picks it up and reads the cover, and protests: "This is the most important one here; it has color photographs and it's all about medicine." Chele says Latina was the one who rejected it, saying it's a sinful book because it shows naked men and women. Chele reminds her that Latina doesn't believe in those medicines, because her blue herbal waters are all she needs. Crista-child insists that he give it to her, that she'll hide it so that no one else can look at it. "If you want it, then here; but you're barely ten years old. You won't even be allowed to look at it. You'll have to give it to Magdalena, but don't say anything to your mother about this," he tells the little girl who, seized with curiosity, can't stop examining the book, her cat-like eyes shimmering and locked in a riveting gaze; she's like a cat, ever fearful and on guard, except that in this instance she's ready to pounce, and it shows in her look. The beauty of both sisters is concentrated in their eyes.

THE YOUNGER daughter doesn't like being in Chele's company; her mother warned her that she had to be careful where men were concerned because they presented the worst danger of all for an innocent girl. "All of us have our day, but it's not your time yet; for now, you've got to keep your distance from men," Latina tells her. Magda, for her part, is delighted; she's smiling and her eyes are as big and white as the wings of a dove as she surveys the covers of the various books scattered on the floor. Her serene eyes, unlike those of her younger sister, are a mahogany color, or light brown, depending on the angle of the sun's rays.

It was during that time that she met Nicolás. The butterflies in her womb were telling her that her body and her heart required the companionship of a man. "It's a natural thing, hija; you're not going to live your whole life in this solitude." Every woman experiences those feelings. Men, too. And that meant danger; that's when a mother loses her daughters. "You're at the point in your life when you're growing up; that explains everything." She had her reasons for imparting the fear of men to her two daughters. "Magda, maybe I've exaggerated a little. Not all men are bad."

I begged God to take away my memories of Magda and He answered my prayer. If He's bringing her back into my head again now, then there's got to be a reason for it.

"I don't know why some people hate flowers," Crista tells her mother as they clear the weeds from the spot where her sister is buried. Their glances cross: one pair of dark eyes, the other coffee-colored. "They're so pretty and they smell so good," she says, referring to the roses.

"Women like flowers, but men don't," Latina says.

"It has nothing to do with being a man or a woman," Crista answers.

The grandmother, evading the issue: "The truth is that a person shouldn't waste time on flowers or things like that; having a clean conscience, that's what counts in life."

"There's time for everything *in the Lord's vineyard*," Crista says, still hoping to convince her mother she's not wasting her time when she reads books in the privy.

The younger daughter rarely smiles. All because she refuses to let anyone know how she really feels inside. Her eyes can't hide what she'd like to keep secret; basically, she's happy, and so they're always aglow, but they refuse to lay bare her soul.

"Flowers are probably important for men as well as women when a person feels happy," Latina reflects.

A short time later, Lluvia came running, shouting that Juan Bautista was sitting on top of the well, with his feet dangling inside, and that he wanted to go look for the stars. The two women took off running, with Lluvia following behind.

"I've been telling you there's something wrong with that child," Crista says.

When they reached the well, the boy was still sitting there, motionless; Latina, fearful of getting too close, tells him he mustn't jump. "Muchachito, what's the matter?" she asks, her eyes filled with tears, and praying he'll get down. "He won't jump; he's playing; this is what comes of pampering him so much," Crista whispers while the grandmother is murmuring words addressed to God.

"He says he's going to throw himself in because he doesn't have a mama or a papa," Lluvia tells them, caressing her butterflies as if they held the secret for the child not to carry out his threats. No one dares to move any closer for fear of making him jump. Juan Bautista tells them he won't get down until they tell him who his mother really is. The three of them keep their distance. Only Latina can save him. "Mama, what did you tell him?" Crista asks. "That neither

Magdalena nor Nicolás were his parents." "But, why lie about it, mama?" Latina ponders for a moment. All the while her eyes are fixed on the child. "Because he came right out and told me he meets Magdalena in the privy."

Crista: "I just knew something crazy was going to happen to him."

Lluvia's presence had provoked what neither of the two women wanted to remember. Magdalena had been resuscitated, neutralizing the effect of their nightly dosage of herbal waters. As they were talking, Lluvia approaches the well, speaking sweet, gentle words to Juan Bautista.

"What's the matter, muchachito? Such a pretty boy, so sweet, like a little Castilian dove." And other pleasant words to that effect which get the child's attention.

"Hija, what do you mean, you knew something crazy was going to happen to him?" Latina asks her daughter. Crista: *So much pretending and so much shielding of our pains; a child can't endure that. That's why I preferred to keep my distance from him, not to lie to him; for me, he's invisible.* "No one's trying to stop you from saying what you think about your *hermano,*" Latina says. "You know very well he's not my *brother,*" the daughter retorts. "This is no time for arguing; we have to save him," the mother says, even more concerned in the face of what her daughter had just declared. In the meantime, Lluvia, still speaking gentle words to Juan Bautista, has reached the well and rests her arms on the boy's thighs; she strokes his curly hair, kisses him as if she were his *madre-niña.* A child-mother.

Crista, in the face of Latina's question: "I mean exactly what you heard me say. Bautista's crazy."

The mother, feeling offended: "If he's crazy, it's because he's gotten it from you, because whatever I am, I know I'm not crazy." "It could be something he inherited from his father," Crista remarks. That was something Latina had never wanted to admit: that the child was the work of two people.

As the two women draw closer to the well, they see that Lluvia has managed to grab hold of Juan Bautista, and is stroking his curls, while he, hypnotized, turns his eyes towards the butterflies in Lluvia's hair. Bautista lets her pull him down to the ground.

Latina is crying. "The truth is we're the ones who're crazy." The mother embraces that idea as a lesser evil because she could never accept the thought that Juan Bautista carries the blood of some man in his veins.

IT WAS LATINA who had taught Juan Bautista the few things he knew. Among them, that business about the stars. *I finally decided to talk.* Crista sees that Doctor Febles was right, that the child would speak once he lost his baby teeth. "The one who got him to talk was Lluvia," Latina affirms.

My grandmother says my mother died the same day I was born. It was a secret she thought she would keep her whole life, pretending to be the boy's mother. "But, since I'm so old and cranky, I like being your grandmother better." *I tell him the truth: that Magdalena isn't his mother.* "The one who raises a child and teaches him, she's the mother." Then she adds: "That's me. You don't need a mama." *As the mother of two girls, I was able to give you what they couldn't. I became your mother.* She'd rather not insist for fear of provoking an embarrassing situation.

Ever since she told me Magdalena wasn't my mother, I've refused to talk. I've kept silent, just listening to her, watching her from a distance. But she lets me put some roses out behind the patio for her. "Who's my papa?" *Ever since then I thought I wasn't going to say a word, even though they said I didn't know how to talk or that I was invisible, or crazy.* "You never had a father," she told him.

I'd rather live in a family. The living and the dead together in the same house.

Then, I ask myself why my mama doesn't live with us. The question is only meant for me because the last time I asked her about it she said she was going to put salt on my tongue. "You've got me worried with all the things you imagine. What's going to become of you if you keep on like this?" *It's because I'm not like other children. I don't understand anything. I can see she's really upset with me. I'm upset, too, knowing I'm so different from the rest. I feel sad not knowing who I am. What would happen to me without Latina? Two things worry me: whether or not I'm crazy and if I'm going to heaven like all the other children or if I'll end up in hell for my sins. I don't want to go to heaven even if it's a nice place, but something tells me that for me to go to heaven, I'll have to be dead and buried. I don't want to end up like Plutón and Magdalena, living under the ground. As far as I'm concerned, heaven is a place where a person gets punished, where you pay for the way you've behaved in life.*

Good people go there, too. Maybe heaven is the good person's hell.

When I want to know about these things, Latina tells me to be quiet. Crista, as part of my punishment, doesn't look at me and Lluvia says I'm a little boy who blurts out certain things without understanding what I'm saying and that everything I say is made up; she listens to me, but she doesn't believe me. When I tell Lluvia all this, she says maybe Crista's right, that I'm invisible, that I don't exist. And I begin to cry, but to myself because I can see no one realizes that one of these days I won't be around anymore.

That was when he decided he wanted to throw himself inside the well.

"I love you, but you have to listen to me," Latina says. "It'd be better if you'd play some games like other children do." She shows him the game she learned when she was a little girl and taught to Magdalena, *who is my mother.* You have to squeeze your eyes shut with your fingers and that changes the world you see.

If I squeeze my left eye, I can see Magdalena and if I squeeze my right eye, I see Nicolás. It all depends on the amount of pressure you put on your eyes.

She places her fingers over Juan Bautista's eyelids; he's

thrilled to be close to her, delighted to play along in order to feel his grandmother's soft skin, *touching my hands. I wish I could play this game with my sister Crista. I love Crista, but she doesn't like me.* All he had to do was look at her, without even saying a word: "I already told you, you're invisible and that's why I can't see or hear you." *What was my mother like*? Some day he'd be able to explain the game he played with the stars to another generation. That's how memories are preserved, from one person to the next. Time is an endless circle, a never-ending chain.

All he had was Latina and Chocolate; now Lluvia had been added to the group, even though he wasn't sure about her. Why are the grandmother and Lluvia always sweeping up? If not inside the house, then in the patio. Sometimes it was Lluvia; other times it was Latina. Sweeping the patio ingratiates a person with the trees; a clean patio attracts the birds and the trees seem to come alive. *What happens to Lluvia's butterflies at night*?

Juan Bautista decided it was his duty to pass the secret of the stars on to Lluvia. *Because I'll never have children of my own to explain it to.* "How can anyone possibly see the stars before it gets dark?" she asks. Juan Bautista has begun speaking again, but it's hard for the little girl to understand his words. "Those aren't stars," she asserts. "If I say they're stars, it's because they are." "Muchachito, you're crazy." And when Lluvia tells Latina she can understand her grandson, the grandmother joyfully replies, "That's because you're one of us." The little girl reaffirms what she said, that he can talk. The grandmother opens her eyes, showing surprise, but she doesn't need to go see for herself.

Doctor Luis Febles said that it was only a question of time; once he lost his baby teeth by age six, he'd find his tongue again. A whole year had gone by without the child speaking, his only communication being with his dog, the trees, and the grandmother. And the stones in the *asoleadero*.

He recalls what he had heard one night from behind the partition where Latina and Crista sleep. "We've got to tell him about his mother, that she's not buried behind the patio, so that he doesn't end up going crazy if he figures it out for himself." Or maybe it had been a dream. In any case, the next day Latina would confirm what he had heard and from then on he was no longer able to talk. Or he refused. "Dear God, what's gotten into that child?" The grandmother thought it was some bad seed in the boy that made him refuse to answer her. "Suddenly it's as if he's lost his tongue," she tells Crista, who says that Bautista has more tricks than the devil.

THE CHILD had already been asking me at an early age about who his mother was and I told him I was. Bautista: "You're my grandmother." Latina: "I'm your mama and your *abuela.* The one who feeds you and keeps you alive is your mother, and I'm the one who does that." *Even though I didn't want to mention her name, I told him that Magda was his mother.* Given that illusion, he gradually came to believe he was meeting her behind the house, inside the privy. Bautista: *I kept thinking maybe I didn't need a mother if I had a grandmother. Mothers love their children; I've seen that.* The iguanas guard their babies so that some hawk doesn't carry them off; and the hen doesn't let anyone get near her chicks, and she'll fight off her enemies. In the same way, then, a grandmother is like a mother. Latina: *And he asks me who his father was. I tell him I'm his mama and papa all in one. That there never were any men in his family except him.* "You're too little to understand these things," she tells him.

And every day that passes he's getting things out of me he shouldn't know about, things that could affect him in some way the rest of his life. "And what about Nicolás; isn't he part of the family?" he asks. "Child, you've got to learn not to pester." It was best to forget all those sad stories. And she gives him a big hug, enough to make him stop asking about Nicolás for the time being.

WHERE DID the stars go after five o'clock in the morning? Why can't a person see them during the day? He needed something to negate his boredom, to have some kind of companionship. Latina doesn't answer him because sometimes she isn't in the mood, or it takes such an effort to make sense of his garbled words. Besides, Juan Bautista liked to repeat the same things over and over.

"Muchachito, you're trying my patience." And then to herself: *There are certain people who grab hold of a thing and just beat it to death.* "All right, I'll tell you for the last time and I want you to get it through your head: stop asking me the same question." And she has to explain to him that there're no stars in the well water. "They don't exist down there." And not to lean over the edge of the well either. Then, she chases him out.

Grandmother and grandson, sitting on the boulders in the *asoleadero.* Burning rocks from the Siramá River, like so many thousands of suns stacked on top of each other. Both are seated on a piece of cloth so they won't cook their bottoms on the sizzling meteors. At noon, every rock is like a sun. White, gray and blue rocks.

He learned to see the stars by pressing his fingers against his eyes. Latina urged him on "so you don't go crazy, so you'll see how those stars aren't real; they're only real in your imagination." A person's body, like the universe, was filled with suns and milky ways; that was the idea he got from their little game and that was the universe he liked to imagine. Each individual body a universe, even though the word itself frightened him just as much as that other word: "hell". It didn't matter to him if the stars were real or not. In any event, his reality was better than Crista's or his grandmother's reality. Because he could lock himself inside the privy with Magdalena even if no one believed him.

"HOW COULD so many stars fit inside a pool of water?" Bautista asks Latina. Which water did he mean? The water of the rivers, of the seas? To Bautista's mind the sky is an ocean of water. Latina explains: "The most important thing is that the water has to be calm and hidden in the shadows, like the well water; that way it can be a home for the stars."

"The stars come down out of the sky through the rivers of rainwater and hide themselves in that black hole where moss and fern grow," she tells him. And he, hauling up the water everyday, how come he had never seen them before? he wants to know. Because he wasn't tall enough to see over the ledge of the well and look down inside. His only job was to lower the bucket and pull it back up by the henequen rope. When he turned five, he had been handed the chore of hauling water from the well. "In this life, all of us work when it's necessary," he can hear Latina saying. Now he and Lluvia take turns.

Latina: "They're there even if you don't believe it because they make themselves so small." Tiny stars, like little toys. That's why it's so hard to find them during the day. "But, don't ever try to prove it to yourself by looking inside the well."

"Why didn't you tell me before that they're there?" he asks. Latina explains to him that people shouldn't be so curious: "Just think: suppose I'd told you about it and you went there, wanting to see them; imagine the risk you'd be taking, leaning over the well like that." And he keeps wanting to know more about the stars: "Then what happens to them?" Latina: "They're inside a person's blood, in his eyes. That's where you ought to look for them and not in the water."

She had seen him sprawled out on top of the well, on the stone ledge, shouting "stars, stars". Then: "In the name of God Almighty! Don't ever do that again as long as you live; suppose you fell in." That's when Latina got the idea for the little game, getting him to shut his eyes tight with his fingers. "Now you'll be able to see the stars without risking your life." Not long afterwards, Juan Bautista realized that with that same technique he could also see people who had disappeared, including Magdalena.

By squeezing his eyes shut, he also transformed the grandmother into a *pájaro de fuego*, a firebird. Especially when she was smoking her Honduran *puros*. In that way, he never felt abandoned, even though at times it seemed the house was actually too big for the four of them, including the *chucho*, Chocolate. *My grandmother looks orange.* When she would start smoking, always after five in the afternoon, Latina and her ankle-length dress turned a reddish color; the hour of the day when the incandescent sun disappeared into the mouth of the Chaparrastique.

Latina's eyes are bathed with tears. And Bautista asks her why she's crying. "Old women like me start to act silly at our age," she says. "Abuela, why did you say Magdalena isn't my mother?" Latina grows impatient. "Where do you get such ideas?" She had never told him any such thing. Then, to herself: *Besides, whether or not it's true, it's all the same thing. We're tragic people.* And, perhaps for that very reason they were beautiful—the women and the little boy. Even Chocolate. It scares her when she realizes how sometimes the strangest thoughts come to her.

What mattered most to Bautista was that *Magdalena speaks to me, so then, she must be alive.* She made her first appearance days before Lluvia showed up. And that was when he began to articulate his first words and then he tried it out on himself. He had gone mute when Latina told him that Magdalena wasn't his mother, but it was also Magdalena who had given him back his voice. Moreover, she promised him she was going to teach him how to read, using the old newspapers they kept in the *escusado* for toilet paper: "And then next you'll be able to read from the books that Crista keeps under her bed." *I told her about the books in the cardboard boxes Crista kept hidden under her bed.* "Those books were mine; one day we're going to pull them out and read them together," Magdalena had told him.

What pleased him the most was that Magdalena would teach him how to count. And so it was. The two of them together in the privy. First, using his fingers; then as he gradually advanced, he began using his toes until he had run out of digits. Next they used the oranges that hung from the branches. "And in the evening you can practice counting the stars." As they slowly appeared against the sky's cellophane roof. Magdalena also taught him how to climb the orange tree, impossible as it was to scale because of its thick trunk, but it was easier for him to start with the cashew tree whose branches were more flexible, bending under his weight until he was suspended above the branches of the orange tree; that was how he could go from one tree to another. "Where did you learn so many things?" *Death.* That was when he turned six and lost his first baby tooth.

He made a habit of it—counting the stars until there were thousands of them in the darkening sky. Counting them becomes a passion he can't control. Something interrupts him; he hears Latina shouting: "It's time to come in now before the mosquitoes start to eat you up."

But he was having too much fun counting the luminous fireflies; at last, he got up to one thousand. And then he discovered he could count past one thousand one all the way up to one hundred thousand. That was exactly how Crista learned to count when she was a child. He was as fascinated by the real stars as by the imaginary ones he could see when he would shut his eyes tight, counting them one by one as they gradually appeared in his mind's eye.

He sees the night advancing, like a deadly centipede. Inside the house, the reality of four walls made no difference: the centipede penetrated everything. Like a poisonous gas. Neither doors nor bolts can impede it. And again the thought of being buried next to Magdalena came to him; he'd rather be kidnapped by the coyote-dogs or the evil spirits.

IT DOESN'T matter how much time he spends in the privy. The grandmother is the only one who can reprimand him, the only one who respects his privacy, which in itself was a way of giving in to him. Forcing him to come out is a form of pampering, although he doesn't understand it yet; he assumes he's being punished. Of course, Latina almost always gets angry when he puts up a struggle.

Unlike Crista, who has no time for answering questions, he had learned to respect a person's wish not to communicate. As far as Lluvia was concerned, his contact with her was minimal; most of the time it was Magda who occupied his thought. "Why doesn't Crista like me?" he asked. "Of course, she likes you. That's just how she is; she's not the talkative type."

Lluvia: "I love you." Ultimately, even though the little girl's affection held little meaning for him, he was happy to have her around because she let him touch the butterflies in her hair.

He insists on Latina telling him whether or not the stars sail in the sky. The grandmother repeats it to him a thousand and one times, that there are rivers in the sky, but that the sky isn't made of water.

It looks that way when it rains; the rain sails along up

there, but the sky is a cold wind. "Things that seem to be deceive us," she explains. "And what happens to the pee the *azacuanes* make when they fly overhead?" Latina turns impatient: "You're going to be the death of me."

Children are from another world, saying things they know nothing about, saying whatever pops into their heads like dreams that can't be explained. "Why are there more horrible things than beautiful things?" he asks. Latina: "God only knows." She tells him that evil is a greater force than good. "Latina is always exaggerating," says Crista, speaking to Lluvia.

"WHY ARE there some people who go away and never want to come back?" He is conversing with Magdalena now and discovers that her answers are very similar to Latina's. "People never leave; it's that we're the ones who want to be left to ourselves, and then our wish comes true," she tells him.

"And the universe, what's that?" he asks. That's where the stars graze. "And where do the stars live?" They're right there, that flock of blue and green goats. "And dead people, do they keep on growing up?" No, because they turn into spirits; the only thing that grows is the living body. "If men are smarter than monkeys, how come we live down here and the monkeys live in the trees?"

"We got pushed out of the branches and we didn't want to climb back."

"Who pushed us out?" he asks.

"God."

"What's a spirit made of?"

"A puff of air."

And if we can't love ourselves, then who's going to love us?

The stars are everywhere. "Are they like God, then?" Something like that, but more than anything else they're like the imagination. "And what's imagination?" That was something having to do with immortality and adversity; it was something you couldn't see—odorless, transparent. "It's the wind and the water that we breathe and it turns into a vapor that nourishes our brains."

Soon Magdalena says it's time for her to be going and she leaves, hopping over the fences then climbing the mountain of garbage on the adjacent property. *I wave goodbye to her, but she can't see me now.* "If I'm coming back soon, why say goodbye?" she calls to him. *We were going to meet in the privy at the same time because that's when my grandmother goes down to Doña Matilde's store to do some shopping.* "If they see you spending a lot of time out here, they might come and find us together," she had told him. He tells her that Lluvia never comes out to the patio in the morning; she's busy sweeping the rooms and helping to sew on buttons and make buttonholes for Crista, who's out during the day. "And Latina said if I spend a lot of time in the *escusado*, she'd come to get me and pull me out by my hair," he told Magdalena. "I'll leave before she sees me," she says.

He loses sight of Magdalena as she makes her descent on the other side of the mountain of trash. He leaves the privy and walks over to the orange tree. Bautista, now perched comfortably on one of its branches, watches the woman he believed was his mother walking off in the direction of the Chaparrastique.

He remains perfectly still, contemplating the aimless stars as they trace a green streak above what is to him a dark nest of distant and luminous bees.

THEIR WORLD collapsed six years ago, at least until the day the little girl showed up at their door.

It was a beautiful day when Lluvia arrived at her house. Latina remembers it as if it were a dream. "With just one glance, you handled Chocolate." "Maybe it was my *chongo*," she answers. Latina: "A person can tell who's good and who isn't. The heart never lies." Lluvia: "My butterflies surprised the dog." Latina: "I don't know."

Before Lluvia came along, the work was getting harder for Latina; now she felt her load had been lightened. She had stopped talking to the walls and the volcano, but not to the animals; it was her nature, even when Magdalena was living. In the face of horror and loneliness, Lluvia came along and took Magdalena's place and, at least, filled Latina's need to have someone to love.

From her point of view, Lluvia was a blessing: *The volcano brought her to me.* And she made castles in the sky. "You look like my older daughter," she told her, and so she wasn't able to erase Magdalena's image even though she wanted to. After all was said and done, if the memory of her daughter was going to haunt her, then so be it. The presence of the little girl gave her the courage she needed.

"Now that Lluvia's living here, you can't go around naked anymore," she told her grandson. Juan Bautista, at age six, felt for the first time in his life that he wasn't alone in the world. And he put on the shorts Crista had made for him; he feels something itching him. "Why do fleas grow inside people's clothes?" The universe was something larger than just he and Latina. Lluvia was bringing them together.

"The sad thing about life is that when you're left alone, there's no one there to tell you what pretty eyes you have," Latina says. And she loves Lluvia the way she would her own granddaughter. "Your mama and papa disappeared, but we're here to look out for you," she says, reassuring the little girl. Latina feels happy and at peace having someone else to talk to.

"I wonder how long you're going to live here." Latina's tone implies a certainty that it'll be forever. Maybe a lifetime. "I hope you won't want to leave," Latina tells her.

The little girl doesn't answer her; instead, she is looking up at the trees, her eyes riveted on their branches, eager to swing from them. She would like to do things like that—provided it's all right with Latina.

The trees begin swaying mightily as the wind grows louder. "A storm's coming up." With each passing moment, the fury of the clouds and the storm becomes more intense.

The trees in the patio are swaying back and forth—like birds in flight—but they remain firmly rooted. Lluvia's *chongo* is flapping wildly in the wind. She grabs hold of her head. "I don't want the butterflies to escape," she says.

"Take care of them; poor little things; the winds can carry them off," Latina tells her. They were so fragile. "What can you do to save them?" Lluvia: "I don't know." Some of them were flying off into the dusk, but others arrived the next morning, or maybe they were the same ones. She tied her two braids together in the back, exactly where the butterflies had made their nest. She removed the ones that stayed with her through the night and put them in a glass jar so they could get some restful sleep. It doesn't matter anyway since a butterfly's life is as fleeting as that of a flower in the field. "They're like wildflowers; some fly off and others cling to the stems," Crista remarks, seated at her sewing machine.

"For goodness sake! The things children make up," Latina sighs.

The rains are falling gently across the mountains. Horses in the distance. The month of May is approaching with its rains, bringing flowers and changes of color to everything: the patio, the volcano, the sky, the earth, the sea.

The two women are strolling around the patio with the little girl. The grandmother wants Lluvia to be familiar with everything around the house: the well and the clay pots next to it, partially buried so they won't break apart; the bluish gray rocks in the *asoleadero* that at one time were little meteors and that now looked like burned-out stars; the roses, the fruit trees in the sunlight. And the iguanas that make their home under the boulders in the *asoleadero.*

"The marañones, the guayabos, and the jocotes don't need much attention," Crista explains to her, pointing to the fruit trees. "In any case, it's Juan Bautista's job to loosen the dirt around their roots, and once a week he waters them and feeds them some chicken droppings, at least in the summer."

BEYOND THE stone fence, they could see the little cornfields belonging to their neighbors. On one side, the city dump and on the other, the banana fields. "And all this is our *solar,*" Latina says, indicating the boundaries of their property. It gives her so much pleasure to show Lluvia around their place. She looks at the red leaves of the *nance* trees, their branches flying about overhead, standing up against the dark wind. Latina puts her finger in her mouth and moistens it with her tongue; then she raises her hand and for a moment remains absolutely still.

"That's a storm wind blowing; that means the rainy season's coming on, but it's not going to rain yet."

"How do you know that?" Lluvia asks. Because Latina's

finger tells her there's a big storm coming from the north; when that happens, it doesn't rain. She wets her finger again and raises her arm higher, her finger exposed to the full force of the wind. The poor people's statue of liberty.

"How can you tell if it's going to rain or not rain?"

When the wind blows westward from the volcano, the rain is crystal clear and it's a godsend. If it comes from the east, then it's *cabrona* like a grouchy old woman; there'll be lightning, and it'll bring snakes and toads from the gulf, and death; if it comes down from the volcano, then it provides *agua sagrada* for the corn, the flowers, and the fruit trees: the nance, the guayabo and the marañon."

The grandmother tells Lluvia that a strong wind is the only thing that gets Bautista down from the orange tree. "It's better not to look at him when he's up there," she advises her. The little girl tells Latina she already knows that: not to look up at a person when he's up there in a tree because then he can fall and kill himself. Latina's grandson has approached, and she pats him on his curls and rubs her hand across his back. "He likes going around naked, but I sent him inside to get dressed." To put on his shorts, at least, even if he doesn't want to wear a shirt. "In this heat, the poor little thing... But it's one of God's laws! Now that you're here, he has to act like other people." Because this wasn't Paradise where people can go around as big as brass like Adam and Eve.

"Would you like to spend the rest of your life with us?" The way Latina says it sounds like she is narrating the happy ending to a story. She can't hear Lluvia's affirmative reply because the winds drag her words out toward the southern sea. In any event, it was something already understood from the day she arrived, after the lengthy conversation with Crista. "This is your house, too." Latina thinks she is standing in front of Magdalena.

"I promise never to leave," Lluvia answers, unable to hide her happiness.

"We're going to forget that you had a godmother, and you'll be Magdalena the time she first arrived here, when we came from Usulután. The best thing for you to do is to pretend you don't exist as Lluvia anymore."

She thought she had been forsaken, but she felt drawn to Latina as if she were her own grandmother. She would stay, and Latina wouldn't go around asking if anyone knew Lluvia or the godmother. In the end, Crista accepted the little girl. And above those three heads, beautiful thoughts began to swirl.

CRISTA IS EXPLAINING to Lluvia that Bautista's attraction to the well had surfaced when he was a toddler; later on they had given him the chore of hauling up the water for the rose garden. But, because he hated that job, he developed a liking for trees and made himself a nest—a kind of seat—in the highest part of the orange tree where he could sit for hours on end like the birds. "But lately he has gotten this idea into his head about spending a lot of time in the privy." Like the cockroaches.

"He's such a grubby little boy. You've got to make sure he really washes his hands," says Crista. There's always plenty of *jabón de carne de cerdo* in the house. Soap made from pig lard. "That, plus eating and saying your prayers at night—that's the key to staying healthy and to having peace of mind."

Crista had inherited the garden from Magdalena. "No one else but my daughter is allowed to tend the roses," Latina tells her. Even though the mother did help her with the watering and fighting off the infestations of *zompopos*. Each rose cutting was planted in a grooved clay flowerpot; then they set it in the soil and filled it with water so the *zompopos*, which always came out at night, wouldn't destroy the flowers; although sometimes the ants constructed little bridges out of leaves in order to get past the barrier.

Crista and Juan Bautista were the ones most attached to the roses; she, because she was the one who cultivated them and protected them from the *zompopos*; he, because it was his job to water them twice a day. "But, seeing as how you're so helpless, most times I'd rather do it myself," Crista would often tell him. From time to time Crista loses her patience, especially if she finds a broken stem. The grandmother prefers to stay out of it. *I don't like roses.* Because she was in competition with the roses for Crista's affection. And now, Lluvia would also be allowed to tend the roses while Chocolate, Latina, and Chele Pintura remained outside that privileged circle. And for the women, Chele had become their occasional man around the house, helping them out with small chores, but he's only allowed to touch the weeds that grow around the patio; the only time he ever asks for permission to go near the garden is when he has to make a graft; besides, he never enters the house. Latina: "The only pair of pants that'll be worn in my house belong to Juan Bautista."

Crista: "You have all the freedom you want to move about here, but don't go near my roses." And Chele: "That's your business, Crista, but even if I'm no expert when it comes to gardens, I can still help you with the weeding." And Crista: "You've got plenty of work as it is to keep yourself busy around here."

Down deep, she was afraid he'd contaminate her roses, given the fact that Chele was so fond of drink; she felt he must have some impurities in his blood that could damage her roses; besides, he had recently come back from those other worlds, and with who knew how many diseases.

"Roses are very delicate flowers; a person could easily ruin them by just breathing on them or, even worse, by casting an evil look on them," the daughter asserts. "You have to pamper them." Bautista tries not to look at them with an evil eye, but sometimes he pulls on their stems just to irritate Crista and get her upset. *My grandmother says I've got a few crazy notions, but Crista has hers, too.* She believed Juan Bautista to be a destructive child: "That's why I don't trust you."

"Leave him alone. Don't you see that's how children behave at his age?" Latina says. Crista: "He has to start growing up, and soon, so he can give us a hand around here."

He also had to water the saplings: the *limero* that would produce green limes, the *zapote* that would produce its coarse, black-skinned fruit, and the *marañon* that would yield them cashews. Chele had taken the initiative of planting some of the trees himself.

"After they're fully grown, they won't need as much water; the rain'll be enough," Chele explained. And during the dry season, the trees could rely on their own resources to capture the dew gathered on their leaves and the humidity that collected in their roots. Bautista: *If a person could eat roses, I'd have finished them off by now.*

He watered them only because he had to. Still, sometimes he would eat some of the withered rose petals, without Crista or Latina finding out. He liked their bittersweet taste. "Such a hungry child, as if we didn't feed him. Why are you always so hungry?" Maybe he has a tapeworm in his stomach.

They didn't always have enough food, especially if business wasn't so good, when the campesinos weren't buying anything because the coffee harvest was over. "We might be poor, but in this house we always have something to eat," the older daughter would say. Meanwhile her mother was a clever woman who knew how to find edible plants on the land nearby so they could supplement their *arbejas*, and chiles, and a dozen ears of corn. Crista says if Magdalena hadn't seen the possibility for cultivating and selling the roses, they'd have starved.

"Don't exaggerate. Making clothes puts food on the table if you work hard enough at it," Latina says. And Magdalena: "I told myself the only thing we mustn't lose is hope."

"How beautiful you looked the day you came home with that big bunch of roses; someone must have been pruning his garden."

"I was lucky to find them," the older daughter says modestly. That was the day she was coming home from the la Cruz barrio where she had gone to buy some cotton fabric. "I sat out there in the *asoleadero* until it got dark, making small cuttings from the stems until I had more than one hundred future little rose bushes." The rains came, and when the roses flourished, the women were pleased.

"If there's no coffee or cotton, the campesinos have no money." And because the heavy rains fall from May to September, they were going to grow flowers during that period. "Planting roses isn't such a crazy idea; you'll see soon enough how they'll grow." And Latina: "The sun will burn them up before the rains come!"

Magdalena: "It's the only flower that people will buy." Everybody has to take a rose to lay on the altar of the Virgin when they go to church. As she's speaking, the words of a particular song come to mind: *Come and we'll all go, bearing flowers to la Virgen María.* And they'd sell the flowers to the school children who take a rose to class for their pretty teachers who've sacrificed so much for them. Every teacher has a clay vase set out on a pinewood table that serves as her desk.

And the venture turned out well for them. Latina wants to give credit where credit is due: "Now you see. God provides."

"What does He provide?" retorts Magdalena, who can only think about all the hard work it's taken her to maintain a rose garden in the middle of the cruel summer. The older daughter, exasperated: "I might as well offer lilies to swine." That kind of talk scares Latina and she hurriedly crosses herself before lightning strikes her dead. "If it weren't for the well, the patio would be a desert," Magdalena reminds her.

Latina's heart tells her: *What's the harm in swine eating lilies if, after all's said and done, it satisfies their hunger?*

They talk beneath the light of the candle while looking for the crevices where the *zompopos* hide themselves before they come out late at night to feast on the plants.

"Everyone knows that swine have always eaten shit, and for those who eat shit, flowers are poison," Magdalena says.

The mother realizes that the older daughter can hear what she's thinking, but makes no comment about what she said except to offer a rebuke: that when a person talks like that, he'd better make the sign of the cross over his mouth to keep him from evil. Magdalena: "You taught me how to talk that way, using words from the Bible."

VERY EARLY the next morning, Latina set out past the cemetery on her way to Los Ejidos, just a few kilometers from Milagro, to look for Magdalena. She went directly to the plaza where she made inquiry among the townspeople. There they told her a pregnant girl had been selling clothes, but then it got dark before she knew it. "And we asked her to stay the night; *you can't be going home at this late hour*, we said." Because it was dangerous to be out on the road then, even if it was all downhill to Milagro de la Paz, about an hour's walk.

Not long after Latina inquired at several houses, she came to the one where Magdalena had spent the night and they told her about the young girl being dead. She had been lying there for several hours in their *corredor*, where they had given her a place to sleep. "We leave our house open like almost all the others around here, but we don't know why they chose ours." They told her they barely have one room to themselves as it is and "so, we let her sleep outside in the *corredor* that faces the front of the house." She told them that she wasn't afraid, and besides, the weather was turning warm and it was a fresh, starry night.

Latina, sorrowful, accustomed to pain, listens; she cannot even fathom the possibility of comprehending such a mysterious and unjustifiable death even though she had had a presentiment about it. The moment seems to her like any other in her life, an extension of her nightly fears. Before finding her daughter, she thought: *Magdalena will greet me with a smile when she sees me and tell me I shouldn't have worried and come all the way to Los Ejidos looking for her.*

THE DAY before, Magdalena had been feeling her belly, caressing the life inside her; the young girl's dark eyes can see beyond her flesh. "When is it due?" She isn't sure: "I think maybe three weeks." The people: "Judging by the size of your belly, maybe it's twins." Magdalena: "I don't know; it's God's will." "You can't do much walking in your condition. Besides, it's late to be going back to Milagro; the night will overtake you on the road," the neighbors in Los Ejidos told her.

The reality of it is hard for the mother.

"We gave her that *petate* to sleep on. We heard some talk about *los seres desconocidos*, but we thought they'd never come here to bother us, much less kill anybody. At first, we believed it was the work of the coyote-dogs, until we discovered the wounds on her neck." The coroner had determined they were bullet wounds: well-aimed shots that struck her neck from a meter away. The truth is she was marked for death even before any shot was fired. Destiny.

Latina cries, turning a deaf ear to the words of the women who want to console her, all of them talking at the same time, trying to comfort her; but, it was too late. "They might as well have killed me," she tells them. But, when she remembers she has other reasons for living, she crosses herself. "Why us? We've never hurt anybody." Latina knows all too well there's no explanation; while smoothing out the clothes in the girl's basket, she begins caressing her. The neighbors tell her they'll help her wash the girl's body and that they've bought her a new dress.

"From this day on, I'll feel guilty for living," the mother

mumbles. "Maybe we did something bad without realizing it."

My daughter was so pretty. "They even took away the seed that was in her womb." She couldn't understand it. "We'll get a cart for you to go back down to Milagro with her," they tell her.

She carried Magdalena home, cradling her and caressing the unborn grandchild that was kicking inside the daughter's womb. Her motionless head *resting on my legs.* Touching Magdalena's still warm head, Latina sat with her feet dangling off the back of the ox-drawn cart.

When the mother reaches home, Crista is waiting for her, sitting in the open doorway with her elbows on her knees and her hands on her head, wanting to invent her own world, different from the one it had been her lot to inherit, tearful because she knew something terrible had happened; she realized it as soon as she heard the cart squeaking in the distance, bumping over the cobblestone street and hurling its splintered echoes into the foothills of the volcano. She stayed in the doorway of their house until she saw the cart and realized that her mother was bringing her dead sister home.

"I have to tell Nicolás." That was the first thing she thought of.

LATER LATINA visited the Moreira family to give them the news. She knew it made no difference to them, and even though they didn't accept her as a friend, she needed the companionship of other voices, to hear the kind word of a stranger, to feel loved at least once, to hear condolences like the ones expressed to her by the people in Los Ejidos, to know that love still exists among kindred people, no matter what the cost or how difficult the circumstances. They had her come in, mostly because of the terrible, somber expression on her face rather than out of any deference, surmising that something horrendous had happened as they called for Nicolás to come. They felt obligated to do this much for a woman whose strange ways had aroused the worst in them, including their strong opposition to the relationship between their son and Magdalena; they were hard people, but it was that hardness that had enabled them to acquire a piece of property, about half a *manzana* or little more than half an acre in size, where they grew *piña* and *guineos*. Power could only be born of force, the machete, and at the end of a rifle.

Nicolás, who was doing some work around the house, walked over to Latina. Reading her eyes, he immediately asks her: "How did she die?" The mother, despite the obvious, asks him, "How do you know Magdalena's dead?" Nicolás queries her further: "And my son?" Before he broke down, he heard Latina say: "I believe he's dead, too." The Moreiras were indifferent because they did not understand the depth of their son's feelings. Latina smiles condescendingly at her shallow in-laws and leaves.

NICOLÁS TOLD Crista and Latina he wouldn't be attending the funeral, that he knew they didn't care for him; besides he didn't know if he could bear it, that they could expect to see him once the *novenario* had passed. That was how things were; then nine days later the young man came by to offer them his help, to do some work for them around their property, but the mother told him they already had an agreement with Chele, who had just returned from Japan. "And you'll have to excuse me, Nicolás, but now that Magdalena's gone, you don't have any more business with our family. Everything's different now," she tells the young man, not realizing she has launched him on a journey of irreconcilable feelings that would last another hundred years, like an endless spiral.

Ten days after Magdalena's death, when the mother and younger daughter went outside, they found Nicolás hanging from the crossbeam of the well. The mother barely had strength enough to grab her daughter and drag her back inside the house. "Dear God, what's happening to us?" Crista pleads. But the mother doesn't answer; she has lost her power of speech and is squeezing her daughter with all her might. Then, without a word, without tears, they locked themselves inside.

Two hours later Chele was calling to them from the street at the front gate, which was locked. When they don't answer, he jumps over the fence of live *piña* and realizes that the front door is also locked, something they never did. He began shouting to them. He thought something terrible might have happened to the younger daughter and the mother. Then Chele kicked the door in and went directly over to the bed where he found the two women: Latina, lying prostrate, with her eyes closed, and Crista, with her mother's head in her lap, lulling her to sleep. Instead of asking questions, Chele is shouting. Crista said he should leave them alone, that it was their problem, but the man insisted, wanting to know if Latina was dead and trying to break Crista's grip on her mother. "My sister and her child are dead and you never even knew about it." Chele tried with all his strength to pull them apart. "Crista, you're crazy; let go of Latina." And he wants to explain to her why he had come, because of a feeling he had that something had happened to Magdalena: "I never imagined I'd find her dead." "She died ten days ago and my little nephew too, and now go see what Nicolás has done." Chele doesn't know what Nicolás did, if there had been a suicide or a murder.

Chele sees the mother open her eyes, but not respond to anything. "Crista, let go of her." He grabs the young girl around the waist with his arms until he manages to pull them apart. "I need some alcohol to bring Latina to." Crista finally answers, telling him to go look for a bottle of blue herbal waters next to the *fogón*. "It's the only medicine we use." The man runs to the kitchen area at the end of the *corredor*, where he finds the bottle. "Give it to me, Chele," Crista says when he returns, and then she pours the *blue waters* over her mother's head.

And then: "Go to Casamata and tell the comandante what happened here," Crista says while massaging her mother's damp forehead. The man is still bewildered. "What's going on?" he asks, not comprehending the situation. "Go outside to the patio, over by the well," Crista explains. Now it was Nicolás who had become a corpse.

"Help us, Chele. I've lost my daughter," Latina says, finally regaining her voice and imploring him not to leave them by themselves. "You've got to go to the well." Chele hurried outside, blaming himself for staying away for such a long time and leaving them alone like that, and only because Magdalena had been seeing Nicolás.

When he saw that the young man was dead, he went back inside to speak to the two women. Latina told him, "I'll go tell the Moreiras and you go to Casamata; you've got to tell the comandante there's been a death here."

It was Chele who led the authorities to the well where Nicolás was hanging.

When they carried his body away, Crista told her mother, "There's just the two of us now." And that wasn't possible. "We can't just let our lives end like this; we never had grandparents or fathers, we never had a family history; we were deprived of memories; it's just the two of us, alone here with our thoughts."

"Everybody lives his own experience in life," says the

mother. Then Crista tells her she's going to live hers; now that she's fifteen, a new cycle is about to begin, one that she wants to be different. "We're not going to be left all alone in the world."

Latina: "We'll go see Doctor Febles again." Maybe he could give them a remedy to help them forget everything. Crista says she agrees, that they've got to live their lives free of memories, but to accomplish that they'll have to do something. The mother asks her what she intends to do. "Let me think about it good and hard," Crista tells her. That same evening she explains what is on her mind: "Mama, we can't stay shut up in this house. What good are the books Chele gave us if they just stay under the bed? The only time they got used was the little bit that Magdalena and I read them, when we'd be in the *escusado*. Someone should make use of them, somebody from our family who'll outlive us."

The mother thinks her daughter is rambling, that she ought to speak plainly. Crista has already made up her mind: "Mama, I'm going to have a child." The mother tells her that children aren't conceived simply because a person wants to have them; that takes two people. Crista tells her she's already chosen the father. The mother tells her she's crazy, that in this life women don't make that choice. "What's more, you don't even know a man."

"Leave it to me. I'll find one," the younger daughter says. Latina: "Don't tell me you intend to go out to the street to look for a man; I'll never let you do that; you'd be called a *puta*."

Crista calms her down: "Oh, mama, let's forget it; anyway, those of us who were born poor are *putas* from birth." Latina: "Stop it. Just shut up now! There's been enough tragedy in our family without my hearing you talk like that." She says it without realizing that the real meaning of their lives was rooted in all that is tragic.

TWO WEEKS after Magdalena's death, Latina finally found the strength to leave the house and make her rounds of Milagro to sell their bouquets of roses and their clothes, using the basket that had belonged to her older daughter. Once the emotional crisis over Magdalena's death had passed, Crista decided to set her sights on Chele who had started coming around again to do some chores for them. She went out back to call to him: "Can you come inside a minute?" It seemed she had a problem that needed his attention. "Chele, I want you to help me with something." Chele looks into those stealthy, cat-like eyes of hers, eyes perhaps filled with animosity, a certain look he had observed time and again in the younger daughter. "I'm here to help you and Latina out, and now more than ever." Crista tells him she wants to have a child. Chele, who had always been aware of the younger daughter's hostility toward him, is surprised at such an intimate confidence. Thinking that Crista was probably joking around, that it was the result of the painful loss of her sister, he tells her: "Your life has barely gotten started, *hijita.* Not even fifteen years old yet and you want to get hitched to someone."

Crista looks at him with the eyes of a huntress, a look he was familiar with ever since she was little. "I'm not planning to get hitched to anybody," she tells him.

Chele: "Then you can't have a baby; you've got to read the books I gave to you and your sister so you'll understand." She tells him that she has read them and understands everything very well. "In that case, I expect if you tell Latina about this, you'll just cause her one more unhappy experience, like the others the two of you have already suffered." "My mama knows all about it," she replies. "I don't believe it. She wouldn't let you do this. And be that as it may," the man tells her, "I don't know how I can be of any help to you."

Then Crista, riveting her rancorous eyes on him: "I've been thinking about you, Chele."

The man, knowing all too well what she's like, begins to shake: "Crista, I think you haven't been right in the head ever since Magdalena and Nicolás died."

The girl wavers, but without losing sight of her goal: "You're right, but that's exactly the reason I've thought about this."

Chele explains to her: "You're young; someday you'll have a sweetheart; besides, I'm much older than you; I could almost be your papa."

"You're fifteen years older than me; that doesn't matter," Crista answers nimbly, knowing Chele's twice her age.

The man insists she needs to pay a visit to Los Ejidos, to see Doctor Febles: "Because after so much grief, it could be you're sick."

"Let's stop beating around the bush, Chele; I'm a woman and we know how to bear our burdens."

The man tells her he has never thought about becoming a father. Not in his whole life. If he had to tell the truth, during hard times like these, he had no wish to bring a child into the world, "a child I couldn't do anything for, to bring him here only to suffer in this valley of shit and tears."

For some inexplicable reason, even when Chele attributed Crista's proposition to an insane reaction to Magdalena's death, he couldn't stop shaking.

Crista: "That shows you're not a *cabrón* like other men, the way mama and I thought." As she says this, she goes to the back door and shuts it. "Crista, we can't do this. Latina would kill us both and then she herself would die of heartache."

Crista begins taking off her blouse: "I told you she knows

all about it." She removes the bodice that covers her pubescent breasts and fixes her gaze on him. "Crista, I can't; it's crazy; what's more, it takes two people, and I'm just not prepared to do this." The girl takes him by the hand. "You can." Chele perceives a distinct kind of heat, different from the one he had felt before Crista closed the doors: the heat of Milagro de la Paz and of a boiling, red sun—so different from the heat Crista was transmitting. "I don't want to be a father or get mixed up with a young thing like you. Let go." He feels faint. Crista unbuttons her skirt and stands there in her muslin slip. Then, without letting go of Chele, she leads him over to the bed.

"I've been told men don't cry and that they're strong; you're not going to tell me you're so different," Crista says. "That's not it; it's just that I have a lot of affection for you and Latina and I always loved Magdalena, but then Nicolás came along."

"I always knew that and that's why I never forgave you; I even hated you, Chele, because you wanted to take my sister away from us; that's the reason you gave us the books; I didn't forgive Nicolás either, even though my sister knew how to keep their relationship a secret, and when she told mama, I realized she didn't want to abandon us, that she only wanted to add another life to our family."

"Then you're asking me to betray your sister," he tells her.

"This isn't betraying anybody, Chele, because you never had anything to do with Magdalena; and it'll be the same with me. You won't be the father of my child and I won't go live with you." No one was going to know about this nor would he need to feel obligated to her for anything, not even ashamed. Then Crista releases him and removes her slip and underpants. The morning's metallic light pierces through the slats of the door and nestles down into the warmth of the young girl's flesh.

Chele saw her aglow, bathed in copper and wrapped in the fiery radiance of the day. A solitary soul in hell.

Then he realized that the girl standing before him wasn't a young girl at all, but a woman. He felt it in his blood. The cold shiver, which only moments before ran through his body, had transformed itself into a feverish heat, as if hell itself were beginning to scorch him.

Crista's body wasn't trembling at all except for her firm, tender breasts, which quivered ever so slightly from the small tempest of emotions. Chele felt excited and realized his vision was becoming blurred. "Chele, this will be the only time we do it and you won't be the father and neither will I have any need for you afterwards; the only thing I want from you is your *blood*—a child." By the time Crista finished explaining, Chele had lost control of his senses; he throws her down on the bed and, feeling the urgency of his need, he starts to undress. Crista stops him: "Calm down; you don't have to get undressed to give me what I want." But a different emotion was sweeping over Chele now.

He was a reasonable man, but he wasn't made of stone or wood; it had turned into an irresistible situation once he saw the young girl's nakedness before him.

Crista doesn't let Chele take his clothes off, but she allows him to caress her, if that much is necessary, and he, his mind clearer now as to what was happening, promises her, "I'll do as you say, Crista." Crista: "I'm not throwing you out; you can continue coming here, but as far as you're concerned, I'll be someone who doesn't exist." She makes him swear before the image of El Salvadorcito del Mundo that he would fulfill his promise. "When all is said and done, it doesn't take much to be invisible in this world," the girl reiterates. No one knew this better than Chele, who had lived his whole life in Milagro de la Paz.

Rather than endure Crista's fierce gaze or the possibility of Latina's rancor, Chele swore he'd never return to las

Angustias. "That's up to you; you can continue working and eating here," Crista told him.

And so it was. But several years would pass before he returned to Milagro at the end of one of his sea voyages. His blood was calling him again to see the two women; he had kept his promise not to say anything to anyone. He didn't intend to break it. She had made him swear before God and by his word as a man, if there were such a thing as a *man's word.*

He gave her his word. In the heat of his passion and virility, aroused by an act of madness: "We're all crazy."

AT NIGHT, Latina and Crista are getting ready for bed. "I thought Chele wasn't ever coming back here," Latina complains as she draws the last puff on her Copán cigar. "Let him be, mama. He's your friend, and he can be helpful with a few things around here." "I thought he might have died in one of those far-off countries he told us about." Crista rebukes her: How could she regard death so coldly? Latina: "We're so accustomed to losing people around here it no longer seems unusual to us." She pauses. "Whether a person stays or leaves makes no difference to me. We don't need anybody."

Crista says nothing. It doesn't sound like her mother who is talking. Maybe Chele's presence really has her worried. "He's just another man," she says, trying to calm her mother. For Latina, the man's presence is a challenge that will make her put the herbal medicine to a test against certain memories. She didn't want to lose her daughter.

"You know something?" Latina reflects. "Sometimes he asks about Magdalena; I'm happy he still remembers her," the mother says. For Crista, it was nice to know that a stranger like Chele hadn't forgotten her sister, a person she had adored, but she wants to soothe her mother's nerves and appeals to her sentiment: "Let him be. So what if he asks certain questions; she's dead and for him it's his way of bringing her back." The mother draws a deep sigh: "We've already done that with Lluvia."

All in all, Latina is pleased to see that her daughter is able to handle the situation so calmly and keep her distance from Chele. Oblivion, as if the house were shrouded in shadows.

The two women—prisoners inside four walls. They don't sleep. Separated by the cloth partition that divides the room, the children lie awake, encompassed by fear despite having overcome their terror on other occasions over the tremors and the howling of the *coyotes*, or from certain other indefinable dangers. Crista lies awake for a few more minutes with her eyes open. Her mind is rehearsing conversations from the past while she listens to her mother snoring. She wraps herself in the white sheet and tries to sleep; she's at peace, knowing she has her mother next to her. At least, they know they're not going to die tonight.

IT'S NOT just a question of finding a way to rid oneself of fatigue and induce sleep. Oblivion, a bottomless well.

Tonight is like every other night; fear grows more terrible with the darkness. But, Crista dismisses it: "When all is said and done, we're stuck in this world of ours," she tells her mother. "If the animals are afraid, then it's normal for us humans to be afraid, too?" And they go on talking endlessly. "You shouldn't chew so much tobacco, mama."

The daughter has always reproached Latina for that habit and the mother's response is that her *puros* scare off bad thoughts: "We can't let our souls shrivel up and die. Let me chew my tobacco in peace."

Crista's thoughts are fluttering inside her head just like the butterflies in Lluvia's hair when they want to be set free. Eyes wide open, staring out like death.

That was when her mother suddenly brought up the subject of Chele, but only because it frightened her to think that Chele's presence might cause Crista to relive bad memories; that scared her more than the thought that Chele himself might say or do something to bring back Magdalena's memory.

Latina, nearly asleep and snoring now, completes her thought: "But, one thing I know: we're not going to live our lives as slaves to our fears."

How sweet mama is when she talks in her sleep.

Both women, lost in time and space. Latina, in her sleep, shouts into the void: *Even though I have eyes, I can't see for the darkness.*

Why does she have to babble such nonsense at night? It's the night that crushes everything, anyway. "You shouldn't be so worried about memories. If we still remember things, it's only because we're still alive," Crista says.

"Of course, you'll outlive me. You're young. That's the way it is," the mother tells her, speaking from her heart.

Crista can still taste the tea Latina gave her; maybe they should stop taking it. She thinks that to be happy it's enough just to breathe the air, to feel the earth beneath her feet, to tend her roses, to watch the trees grow. "That's why God made us, what He wants from us; we're human, that's what we are," she tells her mother. The only time she thinks about God is when she's lying in bed. As she closes her eyes in an effort to induce sleep, she feels the softness of the white cotton sheet against her skin.

EARS ATTUNED to the darkness. That allows Latina to recreate the past as if it were there, with them. "Lluvia isn't going back to the volcano because she has no one there," the mother tells her. "Oh, for God's sake, don't get me started thinking about Magdalena or Juan Bautista or about Lluvia," Crista replies. Then: "Why's God good to some and not to others?" Latina: "God doesn't choose our path for us. He only points us in a certain direction and then it's up to each one to find his own way, like the *zompopos* that infest our patio." "Then, what's our purpose in living?" the daughter asks.

It's a question that perhaps they'd never be able to answer. Fatigue encompasses their bodies. Cucarachas and fierce ants on their skin. "Death's a crock of shit," Latina says, but she means *life. Sleep and sweet dreams, you give us our only rest.* Because dreams were unreal and perhaps, at the same time, so kind. Certainly it was one thing for them to feel imprisoned by their world, but then quite another to feel that life itself was a prison. Latina: "We shouldn't feel threatened by our memories."

Crista: "Some day we'll live like people from other worlds." Then she crosses herself because she believes that *not accepting what God has granted us is one of the great sins. To hell with other people.* She feels like cursing when there's a full moon. *When that happens, it's best for me to sleep. And my mother goes to get the tea, and I drink it, even though I'm so sleepy.* Crista's eyes grow heavy. *But I can't sleep.*

Wrapped in her white sheet, which is barely discernible because of its fresh, clean smell from the noonday sun, the younger daughter walks over to Juan Bautista's bed, following the path memory dictates so that she won't trip over anything. Bautista is asleep and he hears an anguished cry in the distance. The white sheet spreads itself at the feet of the child, who is dreaming about seeing his mother again.

LLUVIA ALSO has her eyes and ears open. She has heard some of the conversation between Crista and Latina about death. And in the morning, she asks Latina about it. "There's no need for you to feel worried," the mother tells her. "Those are just things Crista makes up when she's troubled about something." When that happens, she likes to be by herself and talk about her nightmares and her fears.

"Anyway, what exactly did you hear?" Latina asks.

"I heard something about Nicolás, about his death."

"It's nothing; I told you who he was."

"Why's Crista worried?" Lluvia asks.

Latina doesn't answer. It frightens her to think that her daughter may be starting to remember certain things.

Lluvia knows there's more to it, but she isn't going to pursue it; at any rate, she can't help but overhear the nightly conversations. Even if she isn't always sure that what she hears is part of her dreams, a thought that at least provides her some measure of calm, she prefers to take refuge in Crista's words: "No one should pay any attention to dreams because they lie and make us believe things that aren't real."

Once Lluvia overcomes her concern, she stops asking about things that make no sense to her. "What really makes me sad is that the butterflies don't want to live in my hair anymore," she tells the mother. Latina: "That's how it is. Your butterflies stay with you only while you're little; we all had butterflies in our hair at one time, but after a while we gradually forget them as we begin feeling other sensations nature gives us." *Then they come to make a nest in your belly.* The little girl draws a deep breath: "I love you so much," she tells Latina. They hug each other tight.

Now that she feels sure of Lluvia's love, Latina decides to tell her the truth about something that has been building up inside her for the last few days. "I always knew who your godmother was, but I never wanted to tell you or Crista, or anybody else." The little girl tells her it no longer matters, that she has a mother now, "and that's you." Matilde had confessed everything to Latina: "She's my godchild, but I thought since the soldiers from Casamata come to my store all the time it would be too risky for the girl to stay with me; besides, seeing her in that cotton dress and with those butterflies in her hair, I thought she was the nicest gift you could have in your loneliness."

"And that day the two of us cried together because of you, Lluvia; and Matilde promised me she'd keep the secret. She told me: Your house is safer for Lluvia because you don't receive visitors." *And what's more, Lluvia made Magdalena come back.*

"WHY'S CRISTA so serious?" Lluvia asks Latina. "She really had a hard time after her sister's death. And then she's always out working and when she gets home, she doesn't feel like talking about anything except her work, and when she's in bed she only wants to be left alone with her thoughts, but she still loves us."

"I know she loves us, but sometimes she talks about death so much it scares me," Lluvia says. "Don't worry; it's only on account of those bad dreams she has," Latina insists.

Lluvia promises her she won't pester her anymore; she was even going to forget about the fact that, for the younger daughter, Juan Bautista was invisible. "Don't forget that she's been taking my herbal remedy," Latina says. "She's had a hard time with everything."

"I promise you I won't worry about anything anymore and I can do it without needing to drink any of those blue waters either," Lluvia replies, referring to the nightly doses of herbal tea she sees the two women take.

Latina: "The tea helps us forget our bad thoughts, but that's something children don't have."

She told Lluvia how her daughters gradually changed into women and that after Magdalena's death, Crista nearly went crazy; she started having bad dreams even when she was just a little girl, and she thought it was all because Crista used to lock herself inside with the books that a friend had given them. That's what happened to her after her sister's death. "The *novenario* for Magdalena's soul was barely over when she came right out with it and told me: *Mama, I don't want us to go on like this by ourselves.*" Threatened by certain indefinable fears, the mother had to do something so they wouldn't agonize every night, but as it turned out those fears became a part of their reality. First, the death of the dog, then Magdalena's death, and finally, Nicolás. "Who'll be next?" Crista wanted to know. "*Los seres desconocidos* won't ever let us live in peace." "What do you want us to do?" Latina asked her. Crista: "Go back to Usulután." That would not have changed anything; besides, after so many years, no one would recognize them and they'd just go on being alone.

"Maybe if we had a man in this house," Latina says, listening to her heart. Crista answered her the way her mother had taught her: "Men are evil." Latina: *All the same, I was crazy enough to hook up with one. And then the two of you were born.*

BAUTISTA IS hauling up water when he begins shouting, "Stars, stars." A shout drenched with the humidity of ferns and moss. Crista runs toward him: "What on earth! Why are you shouting into the well? What a scare you gave me." Bautista: "Because to see them, you have to call them. Why can't I shout at the stars if that's the only way I can see them during the day?"

"Just think what would happen if you fell in. Can't you be patient and wait until they come out at night?"

"What would happen to me if I fell into the well?"

"You'd die, you stupid little boy."

His body trembled. Because the word *death,* like the word *evil,* struck him as dreary and dismal ever since he had first heard them spoken by the two women at night. They were even more frightening to him than the word *sin.* Words that made him shiver; that was the only part of his grandmother he didn't like, her repeated imprecations and threats of eternal damnation.

"What does the word *morir* mean?" he asks Crista.

"*To die* means to sleep under the ground forever. Like Plutón or like Magdalena."

"Or like Nicolás."

"Who's Nicolás?" Crista asks.

If she didn't know, neither did he. He looks up, trying to catch a glimpse of the aimless goshawks that are plowing the sky in lance-like formation.

Bautista rarely says anything to Crista; she doesn't understand him, or that he's bored, and hardly ever tries to get close to him. He wanted to have something that could make him feel happy and that's why he had gone to the well to hang over the ledge and look down at the stars in the water, and then Crista came out with that business about death—a word that would make his body shudder for hours on end unless he managed to get his mind off it with something else. An excessive weight for a heart that was still so small. Like a bird's egg. "I have to mention it because it's a fact of life." Those were Crista's exact words. The same words he had heard at night, at different hours, when Crista and Latina would be talking.

Now he takes up the subject with Lluvia who is able to clarify things for him and rid him of a fear that goes so deep it even clings to his clothes; he gives his shorts a hard tug: "If I look at the stars, I feel happy," he tells Lluvia. She answers him even though she's not in the mood: "Just because a person feels happy, doesn't mean he won't die. Look, you'll see plenty of stars at night. And in just a few hours they'll fill the sky." Moreover, she reminds him that neither Crista nor Latina would put up with him hanging over the edge of the well. "That's one of the things your grandmother made clear to me."

"Lluvia?" Bautista asks softly. He thought he heard her moving behind him in the patio's laundry area. And when he gets no answer at first, he looks around, but there's no one there. He looks again, more closely this time, and realizes that the girl hasn't left her spot behind the laundry tub where she is washing clothes. He shouts to her: "What does the word *morir* mean?" Meanwhile he's lifting a bucket of water and emptying it into a clay pot. Without interrupting his chore, he repeats his question.

Lluvia looks up and sees that he has just finished taking his bath: still naked, evaporating in the summer's vapors. "I think I hear someone calling me, but I can't see anybody." Bautista, fretting, persists in repeating her name: "Lluvia, Lluvia." "I hear a faint voice. Where's it coming from?" she asks again, raising her voice.

In the summer haze, the locusts have flooded the patio with their sounds. "The summer air makes people invisible," she says. He leaves the well and walks over to touch her. "Where does so much steam come from?" he asks her. "It comes from the earth; it's burning up and evaporating," the little girl says in an attempt to find a suitable answer.

"Who's that touching my hands?" Lluvia asks.

"It's me," Bautista replies, looking distressed.

"What a silly little boy; you're always making yourself invisible. Where are you?" she asks. "Right here," he says, patting her dress. Lluvia feels around in the air, and as she continues gesturing with her arms, she tells him: "How many times have I told you not to make yourself invisible!" Maybe because he was naked; that must be why she couldn't see him. He glances down at his body without letting go of Lluvia. "I'm not invisible," he insists. "Then, why can't I see you?"

"I'm right here." She tells him she can't see him, but that she'll find him soon enough. All the while she is imitating the hesitant steps of a blind girl, walking with her arms extended in front of her, searching for him. She moves her hands in circular motions around his head, touches his hair, and then other parts of his body as if she wanted to make a sketch of him. "You're almost nine years old. You can't keep going around naked in front of people," she tells him. A loud sob. "Oh, there you are; it's you, that's for sure." Then, complaining: "It's high time you stop making yourself invisible if you want us to talk." She continues caressing his curls. "It's you, all right," she tells him. "But, either I'm blind or you don't exist. I know what I'll do. I'll kiss your plump little cheeks to see if you change back into a little boy I know."

And she kisses him; meanwhile he strenuously affirms that it really is him, that he does exist, because suddenly he was afraid again, worried if maybe he really was dead because, according to Latina, the only invisible beings in this world are dead people. "Go on now and put your pants on, and quickly before you become invisible again," Lluvia tells him. "Hurry up now, before you disappear." Then, feeling repentant: "Wait." And not letting go of him: "You might disappear again. I'll put your pants on for you." And she leads him by the hand to the *asoleadero* where his little shorts were laid out on the stones to dry.

It was at that moment she realized that the butterflies in her hair had begun frantically fluttering their wings and had finally broken free. "Something has happened," she told Latina afterwards. "It's a sign you're becoming a woman," Latina tells her.

Her wing-like *chongo* had vanished, too. "Abuela, what's happening to me?" Latina explains to her that it's nothing serious. "Don't worry. I'll help you." She puts some water on to heat and then instructs the girl to go inside and get undressed so she can give her a good, warm bath. Lluvia's red blood is an announcement that she will one day have children of her own; she doesn't know when. That's up to nature and its wisdom. "As of today, you've become a woman," Latina calmly tells her, but Lluvia doesn't understand; she has always associated blood with death. "That's how God works through you; He's in your blood." *In your menstrual period.* God turns to blood inside the woman and creates life.

"And so it goes, life and death; it's all one thing together. Someone gives us life and then takes it from us. Don't worry. Crista and I will look after you."

Latina understood that from that point on everything would be different; three generations of women were a great force in the face of inhumanity.

THERE WERE two strong tremors that really made Latina nervous. She was scurrying about the house, sweeping the patio, and making Lluvia hurry to clean up the leaves in the *asoleadero*. Keeping busy like that made her forget her fear of dying—always a living terror for her. The mother is anxious for her daughter to get home. That's why, when she hears Chocolate barking, her heart returns to her chest. A sign that Crista is almost at the corner.

Chocolate senses her a hundred meters away before she reaches the house and hurries to greet her, and to help carry the basket. Just knowing Crista got home alive is reason enough to be happy. Lluvia also goes to greet the younger daughter, glancing back at the grandmother and Juan Bautista.

Squeals of protest. The boy doesn't know how to break his grandmother's grip; she's holding him tight and has his head resting in her lap. Both are sitting in the *asoleadero* on the meteor-like boulders, under the branch of the *nance* tree. He has been subjected for more than an hour to the torture of his grandmother picking the lice out of his hair.

Crista no sooner arrives than she touches Lluvia's head. "What happened to your butterflies?"

"I set them free."

"What for? They looked so beautiful in your hair."

Latina would be able to explain it better.

The daughter asks if anything serious happened, if the children are all right, if the tremors caused any cracks in the walls. Ever since she felt maternal again, Crista's mood has been different, although some degree of anxiety still makes her feel inclined to hide her emotions in front of Juan Bautista and Latina.

"The poor little things nearly died of fright, but they're all right now," the mother reassures her.

Crista frowns as if to ask, *Don't you see how sad you look?*

I don't look sad; I am sad, Latina thinks.

"They don't know about fear." Latina explains to her that they'll feel safer now that there are three grown women in the house. "There's a few good things in this world."

Latina knows they always run the risk of death being so close to the volcano, but that's life. Explosions everywhere under the earth. She ponders the situation and makes an effort to put Crista more at ease: "We have to accept the fact that we can't escape God's judgment." It was implacable. Then, almost with a sigh: "Don't worry; all the volcano does is roar; the dog that barks doesn't bite." As for *los seres desconocidos* and the evil spirits, that was another matter even though they hadn't come around for a long time "as if they knew we'd be here to greet them with clubs." Then: "Nobody knows what can happen. Besides that damn volcano, I have other things on my mind."

They hope for a miracle: that death will stop dogging their footsteps.

"Don't go insulting the volcano, mama; we have to show it respect," Crista says. After a brief pause: "Anyway, I know evil spirits are the devil's work." After another pause, she reflects: *When will these evil spirits stop hanging over us?*

The mother says nothing. She too has been thinking about something, that they can defend themselves against the volcano, but not against wicked men who disguise themselves as animals. She knows this much: they're dealing with real men who no one can identify. There's no *spirit water* that will protect them against men of flesh and blood, men who can think. Latina always built her defenses against unreal enemies: phantoms, *coyotes* that can make themselves invisible, Satan, souls in purgatory. In those instances, her prayers worked; her saints had always protected her: El Salvadorcito del Mundo and the Anima Sola. But when it involved real beings, it was a different story. Latina: *They don't care if we live or don't live, if we sleep next to trash dumps, if we eat or don't eat, if we suffer or die.* Their life had consisted of long, hostile nights, filled with the footsteps of some strange animal and the simple hope that one day all those nights would come to an end. They weren't going to disappear. *Nothing's going to happen to us.* But they had to rely on their own resources; they couldn't count on getting help from some compassionate stranger. And on top of everything else, a wave of tremors had been unleashed. *We have to choose how we'll die.*

And from the birds and the leaves, nothing but silence.

"I CAME by way of a long road, but I wasn't able to get here as quickly as I wanted. I almost fainted from fright, thinking that something terrible could happen to all of you, but luckily, nothing did," Crista says, putting her hands over her heart, which is still pounding inside her chest. She sits down on the rocks in the *asoleadero. If not for Juan Bautista and Lluvia, I wouldn't have any reason for caring what happens to us,* she thinks. Crista doesn't feel like talking; she wants to hear what Latina has to tell her. Lluvia and the boy are watering the roses.

"We're all fine now," Latina tells her.

"Forgive me for not being able to come right away. Poor little *cipotes*, it's probably too much for them."

"For Chocolate, too," Latina says.

"Were you scared?" Crista asks.

"Of course, I was. But God is good and He didn't let any walls fall on top of us; there were, at least, two strong tremors, and a dozen more about the size of chicken turds," Latina tells her. And she looks at her hens that had climbed onto the branches of the *jocote.* "Poor little hens, all you've got is us." When the sky grew dark with the smoke from the exploding Chaparrastique, the hens thought it was time to nestle down for the night. "If it weren't for us, who else would you have in this world to take care of you?" Latina tells them. Then, the birds settled down for a night's sleep on the branches of the *jocote. And who do we have to look after us? We don't need anyone. Nobody owns us. We're free.*

"You can't imagine how the tower clock was teetering," says Crista, touching her head. "When that happens, you can't tell if it's your head or the ground that's trembling."

"They both tremble," says Latina, looking sorrowful.

A person's heart, too, thinks Crista, again placing her hands over her chest, suddenly behaving more like a mother, although she isn't consciously aware of what she's doing. It still hasn't completely dawned on her that she has two children: one of them, blood of her blood, Juan Bautista, and the other, Lluvia, legacy of Magdalena's spirit.

"When the volcano rumbles, it sounds like airplanes dropping bombs," says the grandmother, crossing herself.

"The volcano won't let us live in peace with its awful noise; I hope a wall doesn't come down on top of us," Crista remarks.

"And just to make things worse, Chele's back after traveling over all those oceans he invents," Latina adds.

"I erased him from my mind a long time ago," Crista says calmly, in contrast to her mother's mood.

"After all it took for you to forget everything, you'll need to start all over."

"I don't care," the daughter replies, but without her usual resolve.

"After what he did to you, he's not welcome in this house," Latina says angrily.

"He didn't do anything to me; he did what I wanted him to do." And she lets her mother know that the herbal tea that was supposed to make them forget the past never did work for her. "I only used it for one thing—so I could imagine myself in a world that was mine and mine alone."

UNDER AN afternoon sky darkened by the smoke from the Chaparrastique's eruptions. Latina: "There's no name for some of the things Juan Bautista does." Crista tells the mother it'd be better to discuss her son's problems in private, the way they normally did. *When I refused to admit he existed.*

"What did he do to you, anyway?" the daughter wants to know. Confronted by Crista's question, the mother turns pensive for a moment, as if she had gone mute, but then she manages to reply: "Nothing."

"Tell me, because you've already put my nerves on edge with this big mystery of yours," Crista retorts. But Latina would rather not force the issue and so both women go off to themselves. Then Latina realized the reply she had given Crista gave her some room to wriggle out of the corner she was in, to invent a lie.

Crista looked out at the volcano as if she feared it would suddenly launch another bombardment. Meanwhile, the grandmother, sensing the early evening air, pulls out a cigar from her apron pocket. It's a pretext for biding her time in order to invent her story. Then: "He wanted to know if the generals have lice too, like him," she tells her daughter, referring to the country's presidents. Sometimes Latina can behave like a little girl inside a woman's body. "And what did you say?" Crista asks. "I told him "yes", that the generals have lice too, the same as him; that in this life, we've all got them."

Peals of laughter from Crista as she watches the day

come to a close. Latina: "The walls of these houses could come tumbling down around this cipote one day and he'd still be talking nonsense." Crista knows, however, that her mother is lying; she doesn't believe Bautista said that, but she wants to keep things pleasant so the day can end on a bright note. Suddenly, Crista's body shivers with the arrival of a cold wind that has come down from the Chaparrastique, or it could be she has a feeling that her mother no longer belongs to her.

Crista looks out at the volcano again; its trail of smoke—like a tongue—begins to consume the shimmering sun which seems to bob up and down before disappearing behind the Chaparrastique's crater. Everyone is still trembling.

She'd like to lay her fears aside. "A person can't be making jokes about the generals, or about death, and much less about God's punishment." Crista says it with her characteristic seriousness, but she makes it sound more like a suggestion than anything else. For the first time in years, there was laughter on her lips, etched there like a perpetual streak of lightning.

"TONIGHT WE'LL sleep outside again, on the patio," Crista says. "We'll be all right."

Latina: "It's not just the Chaparrastique's tremors that worry me, but the snakes and the scorpions that can be hiding in the bushes."

The daughter says that she is more afraid of a wall falling in on their heads. "The children are scared, that's for sure, but I don't want to die buried alive here."

She looks out of the corner of her eye to the west where the afternoon sun has knifed through the volcano's crater.

"Lluvia spoke to the Chaparrastique; they say it's a secret: that a virgin child will speak to that animal," Latina tells her daughter.

"Mama, you, always with a new secret," says Crista.

"And you, always suspicious; they're not secrets; they're things everybody knows." A brief silence.

Latina: "What a horrible day it's been, all these explosions from the Chaparrastique." *But, at least, we're all right. Nothing's new, only a small problem with Bautista who doesn't have any regard for God's justice.* Then Latina decides to tell Crista the truth. "What he said was something about a *violación*; at his age, he shouldn't even have to know a word like that; I lied when I told you he asked that thing about the presidents." Latina is itching to tell her it was Chele who mentioned that awful word: *rape.* And when Bautista asked her what it meant, that was the last straw. But, the thing that surprised her the most was how it could have even occurred to Juan Bautista to speak of such an unholy thing, and at the very moment the Chaparrastique was spouting off, without the slightest regard for the anger of the Lord. "Stop worrying about it, mama. The truth is you really like Chele." Latina protests; she has no reason at all for liking the man. "Time was, when you were a little girl of ten, that you hated him, and now it seems as if you want to defend him. Of course, in my heart I don't want to bear him any anger." She pauses.

Then, fervently: "I always held Chele in high regard, but after all that happened between the two of you, it doesn't seem right he should come back here and offer us his help again." "Let him be; he's a part of Bautista's life." "I thought you'd always hate him," the mother says. "Why?" asks the daughter, recovering her composure. "It'd only be natural after what he did to you," Latina tells her. "He never did anything to me." "Try to remember," the mother insists. Crista: "I remember everything, but I never wanted you to know that I remembered. I didn't want to disappoint you about the herbal tea, although it helped me when I needed to get some rest."

It made little difference to Crista whether or not she remembered exactly how she had finally come to accept the idea that she was a mother: "I believe I gradually reclaimed my son a little bit each night." Wrapped in her white blanket. "If Chele had raped me, I'd have told you," she confidently affirms. She reproaches her mother: "So, you can get that idea out of your head." Latina, dumbfounded: "When have we ever discussed the subject of rape? This is the first time I've brought it up." Crista recriminates her for her loss of memory. "For your part, it was your way of excusing a crime that never happened. Maybe I should have talked to you about it, but I was still a young girl who hoped her mother would have some compassion." That comforted Latina; obviously, her daughter had accepted Bautista as a small price to pay.

The medicine had served them as a benevolent sort of deception. "In any case, we owe our lives to it," Crista says. Then, with conviction: "Mama, if we've no memories, that means we're dead. Then no one will be able to love us." That would be like a living hell. "We're all alone, but we're alive." And they had had their fill of repressing their fears. "The day we have no memory of anything, we'll be dead."

WHEN CHELE Pintura arrived, Bautista ran outside to greet him so he could say he was sorry for all the trouble he had caused him with his grandmother, and all because he felt he had to tell a lie, without thinking about the consequences; and he asks Chele to forgive him; moreover, he wanted Chele to know about all this before Latina saw him. "And why are you warning me?" "My grandmother's upset with you." "What was it you told Latina, anyway?" Bautista tells him the truth, that he told a lie. It wasn't Chele who mentioned the word *rape.* "Children shouldn't tell lies; you have to behave yourself around your grandmother or you'll get your mouth washed out with soap. At your age, you shouldn't even know such words, much less repeat them." "You're not angry with me?" Bautista asks, but he doesn't tell Chele everything he is learning from the books he's been reading in secret ever since Magdalena taught him how to read, back there in the privy. Chele didn't believe that business about Magdalena anymore than the women of the house did, but he didn't want to contradict Juan Bautista: "Where did you learn that word *violación*, anyway?" Chele asks. Juan Bautista explains how he had heard it on nights when there were terrible storms and everybody was afraid.

Bautista's lie didn't matter to Chele. He feels good about being able to talk to him like a son; that was enough for him. Bautista explains to him that at night, while he's sleeping, he hears voices in his head, like someone coming to his bed and whispering in his ear. A shadow wrapped in white sheets. *His imagination has no limits*, Chele thinks.

In any case, he was ready to defend the boy: "Let me talk to Latina. I'll tell her it was something you heard in a dream; she'll listen to me."

And when Chele comes calling, Latina is waiting for him with her sword drawn for battle. "The fact is if you're the one who's been telling that cipote certain things, then as of now consider yourself not welcome here. It's enough that I've forgiven you." Chele tries to persuade her: "Believe me, I never did anything wrong." And Latina: "Don't play innocent with me. You know very well the things that men are capable of doing just because they're men."

Chele tries to evade the subject; he knows what Latina has always thought about men and he wasn't about to add fuel to the fire. He doesn't feel guilty about never having acknowledged the existence of a son who only had a mother and no father. That was how Latina and Crista had wanted it.

BAUTISTA BEGINS to shiver. "Are you cold?" she asks. He says "yes", nodding his head. "Maybe you're catching cold." "No, abuela, I'm not catching cold." It was nothing more than the night air descending on them and soon it would be dark. And with the darkness would come the tremors. "The volcano doesn't have an appointment with Milagro," Latina reassures them.

They decide not to do any work that night. "That's fine with me," Crista says. In the meantime, their hearts are filled with respect and fear as they look up at the Chaparrastique, wrapped in its clouds, then swallowing the sun. They're all sitting outside in the *asoleadero* as the late afternoon shadows slowly creep up on them. Soon, the mosquitoes will begin sucking their blood, but they had no other choice but to sleep outside in the patio.

They went in to get their *petates* and sheets and then arranged their beds on top of the yellow leaves that lay on the ground under the *nance*. But, first, they felt the need to talk about how they would survive this latest threat from the volcano.

It's a night when the stars hang low in the sky. The grandmother lights a bonfire to keep the gnats and the mosquitoes away. The children were delighted because they were going to get to sleep outside, huddled together, near the stones of the *asoleadero*. To scare away any poisonous creatures, Latina arranges a ring of garlic cloves on the ground. A circle of teeth. Even Chocolate can't hide his elation as he paces back and forth between the *petates*, getting himself ready for a good night's sleep. "There are thousands of lights up there just for us," Latina says, looking up at the spectrum of light that has taken on the configuration of a soft lilac, an effect produced by millions of stars.

Before going to sleep, they talk about ordinary things that can be said in the presence of children, conversation children can participate in too. They talk about everything. About other worlds they don't know, places Chele had occasionally described to them, descriptions reconfirmed by the books he had given them.

"Maybe my home no longer exists," Lluvia says suddenly, lying there between the two women. And after a slight hesitation, she corroborates what she said: "Because this is my home now." She says it while looking up at the stars in the sky and with one arm resting under her head for a pillow. "My mother and father are dead." "How do you know?" She would never see them again, she tells them. "They went off to look for my sisters, who were murdered by some men." *Los seres desconocidos* who would never be recognized.

Crista: *What she means is that we've all lied to each other, trying to create our own world.*

"So, you lied to us. You mean to say that no one saw you off when you set out for Milagro?" Crista asks.

"They were with me even though they had disappeared."

They try to sleep, talking less and less, their bodies joined together, fearing God's punishment. They think that maybe the animal-assassins don't exist either.

Latina wonders: "What would happen if Lluvia went back to her home?" Then she answers her own question: "We'd all die." And because Crista has very sharp ears, she manages to hear her mother's muttered words: "Don't say those things, mama; it brings bad luck; we'll feel better about things after we get some sleep." She touches her mother, runs her hand across her skin, across the loins that once gave her life. Latina's white hair sparkles beneath the sky's aqua blue light.

Crista knows from the sound of her mother's breathing that she won't sleep through the night and so she tries to make her feel her presence, feel that as long as they remain close to each other nothing will happen to them. "In the last few days you've been thinking more about death. Why, if we believe in ourselves?" Crista asks her. "Maybe it's the years. We're sad because that's how we are." Then she grumbles: "Bautista goes around repeating words that aren't his; he says he hears voices at night that whisper in his ear." The wind rocks Latina's words back and forth; they glide along like the leaves that fall from the trees. "Don't pay any mind to the things Bautista says," Crista tells her. And then she adds, talking to herself: *All he has is me. What else can I do? I'm his mother and I don't want anything to happen to him. Maybe some nights my memory played tricks on me and I went over to sleep with him.* There's no need to recount all this to her mother because Latina already knows the truth. *She found me one night when she realized there was an empty space in our bed: Crista, where are you?* She was feeling around in the dark and got up to light the candle. She found her sleeping at Juan Bautista's feet.

From that moment on, she too realized that perhaps her herbal tea wasn't working. *My God, what are you doing here? she asked me. I answered her, saying that at night I had certain feelings, feelings about being Juan Bautista's mother. But, the next day we thought we both had dreamed the same thing.*

"THE WORLD belongs to all of us," she hears the voice say. She draws closer to Lluvia to see if she is the one who spoke, but the voices are lost in the night, beyond the violet stars that cast their light down on their heads.

They're alone with their thoughts in the night, wondering about the rumblings from the volcano. They're all awake, but they think they're dreaming.

The two women, back to back. Latina will smoke her Honduran *puro* right up until the last little bit of ash has gone out; Crista's eyes will be wide open for several more hours, absorbing the patio's darkness; her ears attuned to the murmuring that comes out of the depths of the night, noises that sound like a river as they grow more persistent each moment; she knows it's the *zompopos* wanting to devour her roses. The shimmer of distant lights illuminates their bodies, including Chocolate, lying next to them. Their fatigue will be greater than any fear they have of the Chaparrastique and they'll decide to turn a deaf ear to the rumblings from the volcano that's bombarding the Valley of the Siramá River and Milagro de la Paz. They'll stay close together on the *petates* they've spread out on a bed of yellow *nance* leaves. Tomorrow will be just another routine day. "Nothing's changed, but at least we're alive." The only problem was that the constant shelling from the volcano would create a period of dead calm in the streets that would make it more difficult to sell their flowers and their clothes. They would have to wait until November and December, the months when the campesinos return to the fields to harvest the coffee, the sugar cane, and the cotton. But, a person's needs do not wait.

"I NEVER IMAGINED the volcano could be a punishment for the sins of the world," Crista muses aloud. They're lying on their *petates* atop a mattress of yellow leaves. "When it's time for bed, that's when a person should have only good thoughts and stop thinking about bad things," Latina says in her wisdom, finally closing her eyes. The voices she hears are those of the birds and the puffs of smoke from the Chaparrastique; sounds that can be seen, but not touched as they flutter above the family.

They'll eventually drift off to sleep, little by little. *If words can fly, where do they go? With the change of seasons, the azacuanes we see above fly off somewhere, streaking through the sky like an arrow, but what happens to the words we speak?* Crista wonders.

She listens to Latina snoring. Crista is the last one to fall asleep; before she does, she touches Juan Bautista's naked flesh, and he can feel his mother's warm hands resting on his fragile hips, caressing him; still, he isn't sure if it's all part of some dream he can't capture. The younger daughter is happy because recovering her memory means that she exists once more. She touches the child's closed eyelids. She also hears Lluvia's delicate breathing. *The new Magdalena,* my mother says. *Or else, maybe she's the only one,* I say. Crista is certain she won't get any sleep tonight as she tries to discern the music of the stars. Suddenly she hears her mother talking in her sleep, the way she always does: words and more words; words that fly up and cling to the branches of the trees. This time, just like the owls, those fierce-looking creatures of the night.

Glossary

abuela: grandmother; Lluvia uses this as a term of endearment

agave: a type of soft reed taken from the agave plant

agua sagrada: holy or sacred water

aguacate: avocado

aguas azules: literally, "blue waters"

Angustias: literally, Anguish or Sorrows

Anima Sola: A popular religious image among the people in rural areas, not officially recognizes by the Church as a saint, who represents the lost souls burning in hell; a framed painting of her is sold at various festivals.

arbeja: vetch, any herb of the genus *Vicia*

asoleadero: an open area off the patio for drying clothes

assault: This rebellion at the beginning of the 20th century led by the women is a historical fact recorded in the annals of San Miguel

Ave María Purísima: In the name of Mary; Holy Mother of God

azacuán: a goshawk

azufre: a nonmetallic element, yellow in color, used in the manufacture of sulfuric acid

barrio: small neighborhood within a community

cabrón: a vulgar term for someone who behaves badly or stupidly; bastard, swine, jerk, ruffian, a deceived husband

caca: excrement; animal droppings

campo: the country; farmland; the rural area

cancel: typical of the rural areas, a cloth room-divider; a privacy screen decorated with color photos from newspapers and magazines

Casamata: literally, "killing house"
Caza del Casuco: *The Armadillo Hunt*, an old folk song; the soft, white meat of the armadillo and the iguana was a much sought-after commodity
Cerro el Tigre: Tiger Hill: a volcano overlooking the town of Usulután, east of San Salvador, about thirty miles before Milagro de la Paz
Chaparrastique: The San Miguel Volcano that overlooks the city of the same name
chapel: this is the 19th century Medalla Milagrosa chapel of the Sisters of Charity; later a hospital was built around it, which no longer exists
chele: literally "white"; a term referring to any person of light-colored skin and fair hair; more commonly found in the Northwestern regions of El Salvador than in the east where San Miguel is located
chipilín: a green, leafy vegetable with a slightly bitter taste
chongo: an adornment for the hair worn by peasant women; a flowing bow of colorful ribbons
cipote: a little child, **cipota:** a little girl
comandante: military commander; often the local authority
corredor: a walkway, along the outside of the house, covered by a corrugated tin roof that extends over the *fogón* while cooking
coyotes: A common term used in referring to packs of wild dogs or the hungry strays that roam the streets; their faces bear resemblance to a coyote's
cristiano: literally, a Christian; a human being, as opposed to an animal
curandero: a healer who uses natural remedies
doctor: in this case, a "curandero", one who heals with natural remedies

dulce de panela: a soft, conical-shaped sweet in the form of a small vase; made of processed sugar cane wrapped in its leaf which is then peeled back to break off pieces

ejido: government land grants; communal property for farming

escusado: outhouse, privy; typical of rural homes

farsante: a liar, a fabricator

fogón: a rectangular-shaped, waist-high raised cooking platform of heavy wood, set on four sets of cinder blocks, with a wood-fired stone hearth at one end

fustán: a muslin half slip the daughter wears under her night shirt

garrobo: Central American iguana; the male of the species

gobernador: military governor, the local authority

guayabo: guava

guineos: miniature bananas with a very sweet flavor

hierbabuena: mint

hijita: literally "little daughter"; term of affection: sweetheart

hombrecito: literally, "little man"; young man

huacal: used in the rural areas; a small, burnished bowl carved from the hard half-shell of a ripened morro fruit, about the size of a large melon; used by the pre-Columbian peoples for holding liquids as far back as 3,000 B.C.

infierno: literally "hell"; any place of infernal heat

jejenes: gnats

jocote: a large tree, similar to the nance; it provides a fruit popular in the rural areas; something like a plum

la costa: the southeast region of El Salvador where there are small as well as large cotton-growing fields, some as large as 200 acres

La Union: port city 183 km east of San Salvador; about 30 miles southeast of San Miguel (Milagro de la Paz)

lavadero: laundry area of the patio, equipped with a concrete washtub

limero: the lime tree; the lime is more common to Central America

marañón: type of cashew, endemic to Central America; it was one of several foods that provided essential vitamins for pre-Columbian civilizations

milagro: miracle

milpa: indigenous term for "small cornfield"

nance: a large, flowering tree, common to the region; it drops red and yellow leaves when the season turns

niña: female child

niño: child; male child

novenario: a period of nine consecutive days of novenas; a wake

paz: peace

pan dulce: sweet bread

petate: "petat", from the Nahuat language; a sleeping mat woven from soft, thin bamboo strips and which could be rolled up

piña: a green, spiny-needled plant that consists of four to five long, pointed, fibrous leaves that stand straight up; this is from the pineapple family, but it is not the large, edible variety

Púchica: Salvadoran slang; a popular exclamation, but not used in formal settings

puro: a cigar

ruda: rue; oil-yielding plant of the genus *Ruta*, used for medicinal purposes

Salvadorcito del Mundo: a revered depiction of Jesus as an angelic and curly-haired adolescent

seres desconocidos: literally, *unknown beings*; unknown killers, unidentified assassins

solar: a fenced-in plot of ground with trees and plants; a term that can also be used in referring to the house, the patio, and the outdoor laundry and *asoleadero* areas

tacuacines: opossum, from *tacuatzin*, the Nahuat language of the Pipil of El Salvador

tombilla: woven from thin bamboo strips, used by peasants as a suitcase for carrying their clothes on a trip; of varying sizes and with a lid, in the shape of a round basket and often quite colorful

varón: the male of the species; a male child; manly

veranera: any one of a number of flowering green trees

vieja: literally, old woman; the grandmother

the war: probably a reference to the 1932 massacre when General Maximiliano Martínez crushed the Farabundo Martí peasant uprising

zompopos: large, red ants that can destroy a tree in one day

zopes: buzzards

zopilote: buzzard; from the Nahuat *zope*

photograph © by Layle Silbert

MANLIO ARGUETA was born in San Miguel, El Salvador on November 24, 1935. He was a member of the "Generación Comprometida," a group of writers between 1950 and 1956 influenced by Jean Paul Sartre and dedicated to social, cultural and political activism.

His many novels earned him an international reputation and endeared him to the Salvadoran people. They give testimony to the struggles of ordinary Salvadorans against political repression in a style that authentically reproduces the colloquial speech of San Salvador. He is best known in the United States for his novels of social protest: *Un día en la vida (One Day of Life)* 1980, *Cuzcatlán: Donde bate la mar del sur (Cuzcatlán: Where the Southern Sea Beats)* 1986, and *Caperucita en la zona roja (Little Red Riding Hood in the Red Light District)* 1978, which won the Casa de las Américas Prize. His other writings include *En el costado de la luz* (poems), and *El valle de las hermacas* (a novel) which won the Certamen Cultural Centroamercano Award in 1968. His most recent novel is *Siglo de O(g)ro*, 1999.

Because of his outspoken novels, life became increasingly difficult for Argueta in El Salvador during the seventies. He was arrested and expelled from his homeland several times for his involvement in various political causes. After the Salvadoran authorities halted the printing of *One Day of Life* and ordered confiscation of all existing copies in 1980, Argueta went into permanent exile in Costa Rica until the early nineties when he was able to return to El Salvador, following the end of the civil war which had lasted for a dozen years (1980-1992). He currently serves as the Director of Art and Culture at the national university, the University of El Salvador, in San Salvador.

Related Titles from Curbstone Press

Salvadoran Fiction and Nonfiction:

ASHES OF IZALCO, by Claribel Alegría & Darwin Flakoll. Written in two voices, *Ashes of Izalco* is a love story set against the events of 1932 when thirty thousand Indians and peasants were massacred in Izalco, El Salvador. This novel brings together a Salvadoran woman and an American man who together struggle over issues of love, loyalty and socio-political injustices.
$12.95pa ISBN 0-915306-84-0 192pp 5 1/2 x 8 1/2

LITTLE RED RIDING HOOD IN THE RED LIGHT DISTRICT, by Manlio Argueta, translated by Edward Waters Hood. This is Argueta's most popular novel in El Salvador, both among critics and the general population. The story revolves around the relationship between two young lovers, Alfonso and Hormiga, in a time of political upheaval, evoking characters and themes from the classic fairy tale within the wartime environment of El Salvador and its capital, San Salvador.
$14.95pa ISBN 1-880684-32-2 232pp 5 1/2 x 8 1/2

MIGUEL MARMOL, by Roque Dalton; translated by Kathleen Ross & Richard Schaaf. Long considered a classic testimony throughout Latin America, *Miguel Mármol* gives a detailed account of Salvadoran history while telling the interesting and sometimes humorous story of one man's life.
$19.95cl. 0-915306-68-9; $12.95pa. 0-915306-67-0

REBEL RADIO: The Story of El Salvador's Radio Venceremos, by José Ignacio López Vigil, translated by Mark Fried. During El Salvador's civil war, a clandestine radio station, Radio Venceremos, operated in-country by broadcasting in secret mountain locations, constantly on the run from the army. "I did not merely enjoy this book. I reveled in it, from the first page to the last."—Oakland Ross, *The Globe and Mail*
$19.95cl ISBN 1-890684-21-17 288pp incl. photos & maps

CURBSTONE PRESS, INC.

is a non-profit publishing house dedicated to literature that reflects a commitment to social change, with an emphasis on contemporary writing from Latino, Latin American and Vietnamese cultures. Curbstone presents writers who give voice to the unheard in a language that goes beyond denunciation to celebrate, honor and teach. Curbstone builds bridges between its writers and the public – from inner-city to rural areas, colleges to community centers, children to adults. Curbstone seeks out the highest aesthetic expression of the dedication to human rights and intercultural understanding: poetry, testimonies, novels, stories, and children's books.

This mission requires more than just producing books. It requires ensuring that as many people as possible know about these books and read them. To achieve this, a large portion of Curbstone's schedule is dedicated to arranging tours and programs for its authors, working with public school and university teachers to enrich curricula, reaching out to underserved audiences by donating books and conducting readings and community programs, and promoting discussion in the media. It is only through these combined efforts that literature can truly make a difference.

Curbstone Press, like all non-profit presses, depends on the support of individuals, foundations, and government agencies to bring you, the reader, works of literary merit and social significance which might not find a place in profit-driven publishing channels, and to bring the authors and their books into communities across the country. Our sincere thanks to the many individuals who support this endeavor and to the following foundations and government agencies: Adaptec, Josef and Anni Albers Foundation, Connecticut Commission on the Arts, Connecticut Arts Endowment Fund, Connecticut Humanities Council, J.M. Kaplan Fund, Eric Mathieu King Fund, Lannan Foundation, Lawson Valentine Foundation, John D. and Catherine T. MacArthur Foundation, National Endowment for the Arts, Open Society Institute, Puffin Foundation, and the Edward C. & Ann T. Roberts Foundation.

Please support Curbstone's efforts to present the diverse voices and views that make our culture richer. Tax-deductible donations can be made by check or credit card to:

Curbstone Press, 321 Jackson Street, Willimantic, CT 06226
phone: (860) 423-5110 fax: (860) 423-9242
www.curbstone.org